EN

"*Light Ops: The Final Forty* … WOW! I feel as though I have traveled across time and space—personally experiencing incredible possibilities that Vicki Taylor has masterfully detailed. With each hop through time, it's as though these stories are prophetic rather than imagined. A kindred spirit—a connection to our generations—time itself seen from the eyes of the "All Seeing One." What an amazing idea! This book has filled me with renewed hope in the God of Hope. I am left with the question … is anything too hard for our God? To which I emphatically answer: No, Nothing!

I can see this book and its sequels as a series of prophetic movies. I love the words spoken over the redeemed in this book. Warm and Amazing! The pages come alive with truth that resonates deep inside of me in a place of knowing that I feel I've known before. To sum up the book: hope, redemption, freedom from generational chains, new life, deep truths, God given insight and wisdom, exciting, scary, eye opening, and heartwarming. I highly recommend Vicki Taylor's book: *Light Ops: The Final Forty* … and wait anxiously for Vicki's next sequel to her book to come out."

BEN ANDREWS
Pastor | Exchanged Lives Ministries, Peotone, IL

"Vicki Taylor has done a masterful job of capturing the invisible fight that goes on in the realm of darkness in her modern-day Kingdom novel called *Light Ops: The Final Forty*. Vicki has skillfully exposed the works of darkness to God's glorious weapons of light. The reader will gain a wonderful understanding of the power of Christ that is resident within them. They will discover how the angelic realm is used to help believers conquer and overcome all obstacles with the wisdom and majesty of God. You will glean so much from the courts of Heaven through reading this creative, power packed writing. *Light Ops: The Final Forty* is full of revelation knowledge and spiritual insights."

DR. BARBIE L. BREATHITT
Author | Dream Interpretation Coach

"Inside the cover of *Light Ops: The Final Forty*, you'll discover a tapestry that has been woven from vision, truth, and revelatory gems. Vicki Taylor has drawn back the curtain to reveal the unseen angelic war as well as the strategies from Heaven's War Room to ensure victory, regardless of time and space. No battle is lost in God's Kingdom. This book may challenge some thinking and take you outside of some boxes as it leans into the question, 'What if … ?'"

DR. MICHELLE BURKETT
Director | Patricia King's Women in Ministry Network (WIMN)
WIMNglobal.com

"Vicki Taylor has given us a riveting and exciting ride into the end of the age, stories told with great detail of the people in their locations and their circumstances. It gives the reader a sense that these people, along with their angels, exist, somewhere in time. I found that I had an emotional response to this book that came from deep within my spirit every time I sat down to read. It was as if my spirit confirmed these stories. I can't recommend this book enough!"

PASTOR WENDY RODGERS
San Jose, California

LIGHT OPS: THE FINAL FORTY

BOOK ONE

SIGNS IN THE SKY

VICKI A. TAYLOR

LIFEWISE BOOKS

LIGHT OPS: THE FINAL FORTY
SIGNS IN THE SKY

By Vicki A. Taylor

Published by:

⚙ LIFEWISE BOOKS

PO BOX 1072
Pinehurst, TX 77362
LifeWiseBooks.com

To contact the author: VickiATaylor.com

ISBN (Print): 978-1-952247-03-3
ISBN (Ebook): 978-1-952247-04-0

DEDICATION

To my husband, Dan, the love of my life, father of my children, and
dearest friend, and to the One who orchestrated it all.

In memory of my parents,
Donald W. and Peggy A. Seehausen

SPECIAL ACKNOWLEDGEMENTS

My sincerest thanks to:

God, the Father, Jesus, His Son, and the Holy Spirit, for speaking to His children, opening their ears to hear, and for giving the gifts of spiritual sight and imagination.

My children, Daniel Trenton (Trent) Taylor, Christina Sullivan and Autumn Soledad ("Soli") Taylor and Stephanie Anne Taylor, Victor Sanchez and Abigail Wegrzyn.

My sisters, Wendy K. Rodgers and Linda E. Stolz, my sounding boards, confidantes, and closest friends.

Bennett and Mary Andrews, from Exchanged Lives Ministries, Peotone, IL, for their teaching ministry, friendship, and their "writing cottage".

Chuck D. Pierce, from Glory of Zion International, Corinth, TX, for his faithfulness to deliver the Word of the Lord through the Spirit of Prophecy to His tribe.

Barbie Breathitt and Steven Breathitt, from Breath of the Spirit Ministries, for their friendship, encouragement, ministry and prophetic gift, and for ordaining me into the Ministry of the Gospel of Jesus Christ.

Kristina Ingles, my LifeWise editor, whose insights, words of encouragement and thoughtful questions proved invaluable to me.

Charity Bradshaw and her team of editors and designers, from LifeWise Publishing.

Paul Cox, from Aslan's Place, for his teaching on Delta—being stuck in time.

Renny McLean, for his book … *Eternity Invading Time.*

Annetta Sommer and Elizabeth Zacharias, for parallel thoughts.

Annetta Sommer for editing assistance and Lisa Triemstra for infrastructure support, including photo shots and website development.

CONTENTS

"Night's darkness is dissolving away as a new day of destiny dawns. So, we must once and for all strip away what is done in the shadows of darkness, removing it like filthy clothes. And once and for all we clothe ourselves with the radiance of light as our weapon." [1]
(Romans 13:12 TPT)

CAST OF CHARACTERS

(IN ORDER OF APPEARANCE)

Isabella Krieger, Chicago, IL, USA, narrator and scribe – Isabella is one of the 144 stars of light who answered the Special Forces end times call before the foundation of the world. She is the witness to the encounter and will have the details brought to her remembrance shortly after the mission begins. She is the Light Ops Recorder of Deeds who chronicles not only the who, what, and when of mission details but also records the full outcome along the trajectory of each assignment, a task that could encompass more than thousands of years of history. She is 44, married to Joshua and has two children. Her name means "Warrior, Consecrated to God".

Priscilla Graham, London, England – Priscilla is 68 years old, a secondary school teacher all her adult life who retired three years ago. She was born and raised in Auckland, Australia. She was married to Jim Graham, her husband, for forty-three years and was widowed within a year of retirement. They had no children. The most difficult part of the last two years has been a sense of having no purpose in life, which changed once Priscilla was given her marching orders. Her own destiny is intertwined with those of the Light Ops Forces and those they have come to redeem. The name "Priscilla" means "Ancient, belonging to the former times".

Andel Laska, Prague, Czech Republic – Andel works for an information technology company in the Czech Republic. He has been married to his wife, Sophia, for eighteen years and they have two daughters ages fifteen and twelve. He has lived in both communist Czechoslovakia and the free Czech Republic. When Andel was eighteen years of age, Jesus appeared to him in a dream and taught him about State provision versus the provision of God and Andel gave his life up to serve Him from that point on. Andel's name means "God's Messenger, Favor". He is forty-seven years old.

David Eli, New Haven, CT USA – He is a third generation Philosophy professor in the Divinity School at an Ivy League University and a secular Jew. David begins the time frame of his assignment as an atheist and is a "target" for redemption himself in the first days of Light Ops when he becomes one of the Special Forces working with joy for the God who saved him. His name means "Beloved" and "Ascend". He is 56 years old on the day he is born again.

Thomas Agema, Amsterdam, the Netherlands – "Thomas" means "twin" and "Agema" means "Sword". His parents are missionaries and Thomas lived in the wilds of Lesotho, Malawi and Mozambique until he was fifteen years old, when they moved to Amsterdam, the birthplace of his parents. The transition was difficult for him as a teenager as he had nothing in common with the people in this "first world" nation. He is now 29 years old and still thinks and processes in the Zulu language rather than Dutch or English. He is estranged from his parents and angry with their God at the beginning of the assignment and questions how he could have agreed so long ago to be a part of the Special Forces of Light.

Arielle Chevalia, Avignon, France & Sydney, Australia –Arielle is thirty-six years old, born in Avignon, France and currently living in Sydney, Australia. She has been married for eight years to Scott, a physician. She has three children, all under the age of six. She works 24 hours a week as a nurse in ICU at a large hospital in Sydney. Her full name means "Lion of God" and "Knight" and it is prophetic because she is a Knight in the Army of God.

Stephanie Lombardo, Bologna, Italy – Called "Stevie" by her parents, her given name is interpreted "Crowned in Victory". She is sixteen years old, lives and attends secondary school in Bologna, Italy. She has always had a seer anointing and has seen and spoken with angels since she was three years old. By the Holy Spirit, she has witnessed the situations of individuals and is able to give a clear and concise word of knowledge to them as a result. She came to the Lord when she was five years old after she met Him face to face in a dream.

Soledad Perez, San Jose, Costa Rica – Called "Soli", her name means "Solitude", and she is 84 years-old. She is a Sephardic Jew who was born in Costa Rica in 1936. Her parents immigrated to Costa Rica from Poland two years before her birth. The same dream was given to both her mother and father revealing the conflict of World War II that would end all their lives once Germany invaded Poland in 1939. She has been married and widowed twice and has three children. Her last child was born early immediately upon hearing about the death of her first husband. Both Soli and the baby would have died were it not for a visitation by the Lord Jesus, Himself. Now, nearing her eighty-fifth birthday, she has found purpose in her Light Ops assignment.

Isaac Serotti, San Jose, California, USA– just 3 years old and nicknamed Izzy by his parent, Isaac is the youngest member of the Light Ops team. As he is deployed each day, he steps out as a thirty-three-year-old man.

His angels, Daniel and Emma, go with him everywhere as they have since the day he was born. His name means Laughter.

Abigail Zadok, Beersheba, Israel - "Abbi" is from Beersheba, Israel. She was born in Beersheba, Israel, 33 years ago to orthodox Jewish parents, both scholars at universities in Tel Aviv. She came to the Lord after a car accident resulted in severe burns and a loss of function to both arms. A stranger came into her hospital room to pray for her after being supernaturally instructed to do so. Her healing came two days later when she was out of the hospital and her dramatic conversion to Christianity was the result. Her name means "The Father's Joy" and "Righteous".

Launfal MacInnes,Lonnie", Iona, Scotland – Lonnie, as he is called by his family, is nine years old, a fourth grader at the school near Iona, Scotland where he lives. They raise sheep on the family farm just like their ancestors did for more than 250 years. Lonnie has seen and spoken with angels at the same hillock of angels that Columba interacted with them over 1,500 years ago. His name means "Knight" and "Choice One".

Elin Eld, Lulea, Sweden – Elin is 32 years old and a Game Engineer using technology to create electronic games, primarily futuristic games of war. Her name means "Torch of Light" and she is a light bearer in all her Light Ops missions.

Catarina Cruz, Portel, Portugal – Catarina is 19 years old and is a Chemistry student at a nearby university. She lives at home with her widowed father and younger brother. Her first name means "pure" and her surname "cross".

Martell Konig, Herrnhut, Germany – Martell is a 42-year-old man who was born in Herrnhut, Germany and later moved to Frankfort.

Martell is a banker. He is married with three grown children and one grandchild. His name means "Warrior" and "King".

Angelic Host Forces

Bennett – the angelic Light Ops SOCOM (Special Operations Command), War Room of Heaven

Cassie (Prophetess) – Lonnie MacInnes's angel

Christopher – (Christ bearer) – Isabella Krieger's angel

Daniel (God is my judge) – Izzy Serotti's angel

Emma (Whole and Complete) – Izzy Serotti's angel

Trent (Swiftly running) – Isabella Krieger's angel

Zeke (God Strengthens) – Stephanie Lombardo's angel

PRELUDE

BEFORE TIME

The observations of Isabella Krieger, a tiny star in the atmosphere of Heaven:

Everywhere I looked there was clear, pure light, pale, soft, delicate, and luminous shades of every color imaginable and even some that were reserved for Heaven's splendor. Like a September day, the sunlight diffused, as though filtered by a diaphanous film of gossamer webbing over the filter of a camera, whose lens captured in perfection, the radiance of Heaven.

Brightly lit orbs in the most beautiful colors and the smallest glowing stars filled the atmosphere of Heaven. The peace was occasionally interrupted by quiet whispers and laughter from the tiny stars. The orbs were angels who had already been created and the small stars were the human beings not yet formed in the image of the God, Who would create them in His time. There were tiny stars everywhere ... billions of them.

The glory of the Lord was the light. I thought there was nothing more beautiful until I heard His voice speaking to the tiny stars. Warm and deep, the timbre was composed of multiple resonant frequencies like the sounds of thunder, near and far. His was the voice of many waters and it drew me into His arms like a child into his Father's.

I am Isabella and my name means "consecrated to God". I am a witness to the discussion about to occur. None of us to be born in the last generations will remember this conversation, nor will I, until the Lord brings it to my remembrance on a night long from now. My analogies come from the time I will live in, as nothing I am witnessing now will compare to then.

The voice of God spoke into us all. He told us that far, far in time He would initiate a final push to ensure that His plans for all His sons and daughters would be accomplished. He would require help from a small group of us. It was His plan that none of His children would be left behind and miss out on the destiny He had already planned for each of us. We would participate in the final accounting of those that were His and reconciliation to Him for those who were not yet.

Then I heard the voice of the Lord, saying, *"Whom shall I send, and who will go for Us?"* [2]

I heard my own voice answer along with those of 143 others, each with a blink of starlight, "Here am I. Send me!"[3]

Eons and eons later, He would bring it back to my remembrance ...

THE COURTROOMS OF HEAVEN
OUTSIDE OF TIME
1950

"And pulsing from the throne were blinding flashes of lightning, crashes of thunder, and voices. And burning before the throne are seven blazing torches, which represent the seven Spirits of God. And in front of the throne there was pavement like a crystal sea of glass.

Around the throne and on each side stood four living creatures, full of eyes in front and behind. The first living creature resembled a lion, the second an ox, the third had a human face, and the fourth was like an eagle in flight. Each of the four living creatures had six wings, full of eyes all around and under their wings. They worshiped without ceasing, day and night, singing, "Holy, holy, holy is the Lord God, the Almighty! The Was, the Is, and the Coming!"

And whenever the living creatures gave glory, honor, and thanks to the One who is enthroned and who lives forever and ever, the twenty-four elders fell facedown before the one seated on the throne and they worshiped the one who lives forever and ever. And they surrendered their crowns before the throne, singing: "You are worthy, our Lord and God, to receive glory, honor, and power, for you created all things, and by your plan they were created and exist." [4]

Angels fill the gallery, along with the seventy disciples appointed by the original Apostles of Jesus Christ and the airwaves are filled with the voices and instrumental sounds of reverent worship.

Jesus, sitting on a massive gold throne in the throne room of Heaven, addresses the group.

"No man knows the hour of My return. It will be as a thief in the night, the blink of an eye and at a time no one expects. As you all know, wise men know the season and many of the signs have now come to pass. Prophesies in both the Old and New Testaments are already fulfilled, but there are still some that have yet to be fulfilled. Specifically, those in the Books of Ezekiel, Daniel, and Revelation. There will be wars and rumors of wars, as prophesied, but there is one war coming soon that I alone will win. My victory will be the trigger for both the Rapture of My Body of believers—the Ekklesia, and for the Great Tribulation.

"No longer will there be a valley of decision. If a person has not chosen to Follow Me in relationship with me, their decision has been made by default and they will remain on the earth for the Tribulation. Therefore, no decision made is a decision made. The parable of the Wise and Foolish Virgins[5] will be acted out in real life. They can still be saved, as there will be many who knew of Me, but without a relationship with Me. They will be brought home at the End of the Age, if they have not aken the Mark of the Beast or\ recanted their faith, having endured the "wrath to come".

"Please take your seats as we have important business to discuss. We are less than one hundred years out from the immediate signs of the end of the age namely, Ezekiel's War to attempt once again to wipe Israel off the map."

The Throne Room is set up much like an earthly courtroom, with Jesus on His throne in the Judge's position, surrounded by twenty-four smaller gold thrones. Each of these thrones is occupied by one of the twenty-four elders dressed in white robes with crowns of gold upon their heads: Reuben, Simeon, Levy, Issachar, Zebulon, Judah, Gad, Asher, Dan, Naphtali, Joseph and Benjamin representing the people and land of Israel, and Peter, Andrew, Simon the Zealot, Thomas,

Philip, John, James, Judas the son of James, Matthew, Bartholomew, James the younger, Jude and Paul, who represent the Church. All of them are ancient, beards flowing to the ground. While each of their shoulders are a little stooped and the hair white on top of their heads, they are filled with vigor, eyes bright with excitement.

"You have heard the phrase 'as in the days of Noah' and the earth realm is indeed in those days now. Great evil is in the earth, more than ever before, but Noah lived in an especially evil time, as well. Then the Nephilim reigned, angels intermarrying with the daughters of men and creating a no-longer-human race. They were violent, murderous and created chaos. Those on the earth didn't give it a thought, so involved were they in their own pleasures, marrying and giving in marriage. They were so desensitized that evil had become mundane. See it in this time frame. See it in ten years; twenty; fifty years.

Many places, and in fact, as yeast leavens the whole batch of dough, most places on earth will soon be as the days of Sodom. Cultural evangelists extolling the "virtues" of alterations in traditional family values have preached, debated and raged about this gospel and have insisted that right be called wrong and wrong right. Millions of babies have been slaughtered to worship at the altar of self and in the name of convenience. And laws have been changed to render it all legal. Many people have been turned over to Satan with their consciences seared, no longer able to care about true right and wrong.

As you have all read, Paul's letters to Timothy further expound on the thoughts and attitudes of the latter days, but the day is coming soon when I put My stick into the wheels of the bicycle so to speak, a picture of the world on its axis, to stop them from turning. Things, as all have known them, will be no more.

Both Daniel and Ezekiel prophesy about the goat nations in the Middle East, those nations defined as such by their attitude regarding the Beautiful Country, Israel. Those who despise it are categorized as goat nations and those who love it are sheep nations. The enemy hates the nation of My birth and My Father's everlasting love of that nation. He seeks to destroy it. His son, known for millennia as the Antichrist, will soon be in power to attempt to execute the Devil's plans. My Church is keeping her destruction from happening with the prayers of the saints. But even now, as you've witnessed, all nations will desert Israel in her greatest hour of need. That will happen in accordance to the enemy's plan and according to Mine as well, as I alone will be her Defender and will show her all My love and power.

There are prophecies and parables that are converging in time. Ezekiel's War converges with the parable of the wise and foolish virgins. My Body, the Church, must be in full relationship with Me. For those who are not, they will remain behind, forced to endure the Great Tribulation and not recant their faith in spite of the circumstances that they must face. It may mean execution for them but better to enter into My presence in eternity than save their own lives with compromise in a very short, very temporary period of time. It is imperative that they love not their lives to the death on earth and end up spending their eternity in outer darkness. The goal of eternity must set precedence for every breathing moment. Yesterday is no more, and tomorrow is guaranteed to no one on the earth.

Before the foundation of the world, I chose 144 souls to redeem those lost or who would be lost in the last years before the great calling away of the saints—My saints! Their deployment will be soon—in the next 70 years. There have been many years over the course of Earth time that I went down to see the great evils being done for Myself, such as the building of the tower of Babylon. What I saw at the beginning for the end of days, is indeed what will be.

Based on our discussion of the spiritual climate on planet Earth, I would like to proclaim this day that there is a renewed need for the Special Forces deployment assigned to the operation that has been codenamed Light Ops. These troops will traverse the earth and travel backward and forward in time to redeem specific people, people groups and nations in a last-minute harvest of souls that have already been lost or will be imminently. To signify your agreement, please say "Aye". For those who disagree, please state "Nay."

Jesus looked at each of the elders, one at a time for their response. Each in turn stated "Aye"; there were no naysayers.

"Now, let's talk about Ezekiel's War, the trigger." Jesus continued. "As I know you know, the war I am talking about can be found in Ezekiel 38 and 39."

A huge Holy Bible is opened to the Book of Ezekiel and the angel Zadkiel begins to read:

> *And the word of the Lord came to me saying, "Son of man, set your face toward Gog of the land of Magog, the prince of Rosh, Meshech and Tubal, and prophesy against him and say, 'Thus says the Lord God, "Behold, I am against you, O Gog, prince of Rosh, Meshech and Tubal. I will turn you about and put hooks into your jaws, and I will bring you out, and all your army, horses and horsemen, all of them splendidly attired, a great company with buckler and shield, all of them wielding swords; Persia, Ethiopia and Put with them, all of them with shield and helmet; Gomer with all its troops; Beth-togarmah from the remote parts of the north with all its troops—many peoples with you."* [6]

Jesus interprets the verses to the people and gives a geography lesson of earth to describe the logistics in relation to Israel.

13

"Gog defined is the 'man on top', a dictator. Magog is the Hebrew word 'Rosh', which means head. Rosh is Russia and geographically signifies the inhabitants of Scythia initially called Muscovy, modern day Russia, derived from the name Meshech. Ezekiel quotes the words of My Holy Spirit verbatim and writes, 'Behold, I am against thee, O Gog … ' Why would I say that? At the time Russia wasn't even in existence, but if you look at a map directly above Israel, Russia sits almost like an umbrella over her head."

Suddenly a three-dimensional holographic map of the world rises above the table. Jesus narrows the field of vision to the Middle East and then to about 3,000 miles north of Israel.

"I say it because of the anti-God ideology in the nation of Russia. Their national ideology is atheism and no other nation has taken that dominant position. Others have been pantheistic which is also abhorrent to Me but none other has chosen godlessness as the basis for their existence and against Me specifically. Only the foolish would believe that."

Zadkiel quotes a verse in Psalm 14 that states, *"The fool sayeth in his heart there is no God."*[7]

Jesus continues. *"Joseph Stalin once said, 'We have deposed the czars of the earth, and we shall now dethrone the Lord of Heaven.' When Russia put a rocket called Sputnik into space that flew past the moon, and as it neared the sun, the following was heard on Russian radio: 'Our rocket has bypassed the moon. It is nearing the sun. We have not discovered God. We have turned out lights in Heaven that no man will be able to put on again. We are breaking the yoke of the gospel, the opiate of the masses. Let us go forth and Christ shall be relegated to mythology.'*

Did he believe my residence was in the Second Heaven—outer space? I see the end from the beginning, and I take that very personally. I whispered into Ezekiel's ear that I am waiting for that nation and its leaders to do battle with. I AM against him and the spirit of antichrist that is on him.

Ezekiel goes on to say that I, the Lord, will put hooks into Gog's jaws to bring him forth. Those are already in place. Gog needed both the warm waterways and the oil of the Middle East and those were the hooks that have already brought him forth. The third hook is the Dead Sea and all the precious minerals found there. I baited the hook as time began and Gog has come.

The nations are gathering around Israel to destroy it. It is on every News channel on earth and for those who are paying attention, prophecy is being fulfilled in front of their eyes.

> *"Persia, Ethiopia and Put with them, all of them with shield and helmet; Gomer with all its troops; Beth-togarmah from the remote parts of the north with all its troops—many peoples … " [8]*

These are the nations of Persia, known now as Iran, Put, known now as Libya, Gomer, known now as Germany, and Togarmah, known now as Turkey. Ethiopia does not represent the nation currently known as Ethiopia but rather the ancient territory of Ethiopia, areas that are Cushite, as Cush is a nation within the old nation of Ethiopia. These people groups have migrated and now make up the Islamic portions of India, Hindu Cushite, and Pakistan, along with Sudan and Somalia.

The dark alliances were formed eons ago, and while the faces of their leaders have changed over time, the spirits behind them have not. But they will not prevail. Nations that have traditionally honored and supported Israel are turning away, and she is being left all alone. It feels like a betrayal to My people, but that was My intent from long before time began. My strategies spoken in prophecy to Ezekiel and Daniel thousands of years ago will soon come to pass.

The spiritual storm clouds are gathering green-black and roiling on the horizon. Schemes and plans being made in the war rooms of goat nations, those nations that hate Israel and hate Me, and tactics for war are being established. Like a tornado coming quickly, there is little time left to bring people to safety. It is time to gather the remnant into the storm shelter. When the storm arrives, they will be safe and the door will be closed, much like Noah and his family were safe from the storm on the Ark. I, the Bridegroom, will shut the door.

Know this, I will prevail and not one of Mine in the nation of Israel will be hurt or killed. I personally will come against the newest "axis of evil" with My weapons of war, saved in nature from the beginning of time in heavenly storerooms; rain, hail, snow, earthquakes, lava and sulfuric explosions. In My zeal and in My rage, there will be a great earthquake in the land of Israel and every living thing—man, animal, bird and fish—will shake at My presence. The panic, confusion, pestilence and bloodshed will be the sword I use against Gog throughout all the mountains of Israel. I will prevail and it will take months to bury the dead of the enemy nations.

Their unused weapons will be used as fuel. For those who care to search the Scriptures, they will see it has been there in black and white for millennium. I will show Myself strong on behalf of Israel to all of mankind and especially to them. The victory and the revelation of My power and love to My chosen ones will open the door to the 144,000 Jewish virgins, 12,000 from each of the twelve tribes, to be witnesses to the rest of their nation and to the world. All that has been prophesied will come to pass.

Once again, it is imperative that My Special Forces of Light recognize the urgency of the 40-day Mission due to begin soon. All who are seeking after Me have recognized the season for decades, perhaps even one hundred years. My Forces must be able to see the dark clouds gathering on the horizon and discern that the time is near. Every person and nation that belongs to Me must be gathered in before I shut the door.

The nations are My inheritance and at the end of the age and the Great Tribulation, every knee will bow, and every tongue confess that I AM Lord."

Again, the voice of Zadkiel can be heard saying: *"The kingdom of the world has become the kingdom of our God and of his Anointed One! He will reign supreme for an eternity of eternities!"*

The sound of the gavel striking the lectern confirms the proclamation and indicates the end of the meeting in the Courtrooms of Heaven.

CHAPTER 1
THE END FROM THE BEGINNING

SATURDAY, SEPTEMBER 19 – T MINUS 0
(FEAST OF TRUMPETS)
ISABELLA KRIEGER
CHICAGO, IL

The Last Day of the Church Age, moments before the trumpet blast …

I look at the man in front of me covered with dirt and smelling of urine. His eyes are filled with tears, forming muddy streams as they overflow and roll down his cheeks. His toothless grin of joy is as bright as the sun. His coffee has grown cold even as true warmth has touched his heart after years of addiction, homelessness, rejection and isolation.

Suddenly, we are overwhelmed by the blast of trumpets and shofars. The sound seems to come from all directions, ringing like the bells that peeled from every church steeple in Europe the day World War II was declared over, when the day victory for the Allied troops was decreed. In that split second, I realize that the fullness of the Gentiles has just come in. It is possible that this man in front of me is the last. The same man who sleeps in a doorway surrounded by garbage; a street person I pass every day on my way to work; a man I pray for every day but, until now, never stopped to be the tool in God's hand to answer those prayers. This man's destiny converged with Heaven's plans, as did God's appointed timetable for the end of time on the earth. As I look at him, I realize that he has heard it, too, but activity continues on the streets around us as if no one else can. The sound has gone on for a full minute, but it seems to be a call only to those with ears to hear.

I blink and we are transported faster than the speed of light, clean, young again, and filled with joy and wisdom. We are dressed in white robes, brilliant in the reflected Light of the throne and the One who sits upon it. We are the Bride of Christ, in all her beauty.

As I gaze in wonder, I see so many people I know; people I have been separated from for years. Most of them I haven't seen for decades and some that I "know" that I have never met before: my mother and father, both sets of grandparents and great-grandparents, friends, a little cousin who died at three from leukemia, and my own daughter whom I had miscarried at four months. People I have just spoken with at the coffee shop, and those from my church and work are there, too. All of them look to be in their early thirties, far different from how they looked when they left the Earth realm.

I see many others that I have met in the last six weeks. Kathleen and her daughter, and all the generations of daughters that followed, each one with the telltale strawberry mark under their right eye, high on their cheekbones and the multitude of people behind them, mostly comprised of Africans. There is Dr. Porter, his face glowing as he stands with those he has treated and prayed for in the years after he came to know and work with Kathleen. Sayid and the thousands of others saved in Zanzibar during a three-day healing revival are there, as well.

Adan, his wife, Hannah and their children and behind them are all the ones who have been touched by the words of the Savior. Not far beyond them are Atash, Ferozan, Aleksey, Bogdan, and Dmitrij, and the people who have come to know the Lord through the Bibles that have been translated into Pashto and Russian and illegally brought into Afghanistan during the war with Russia.

We are gathered together, a great multitude of saints. In my thoughts, I again thank Yeshua for His great love for His people, knowing that most of those in my line of vision would not be here were it not for the Light Ops assignment of the past six weeks. I thank Him for my part of that assignment, for multiplication, for ripple effects in time and space, and for the greatest gift of all: redemption.

Though we are now outside of time in the heavenly realm with the Father of Lights, His Son, Yeshua, the Savior of the world, and His Holy Spirit; my mind drifts to the day, forty days earlier.

I remember …

CHAPTER 2
AN ORDINARY DAY

"I hear the voice of many angels sing: Worthy is the Lamb" are the words being sung on my iPod as I inhale the intoxicating aroma of freshly brewed coffee while I get ready for work.

I had awakened to the news blaring on my clock radio, all of it horrific. Genocidal and religious wars were raging in five countries across the Middle East and Africa. The projected number of dead people was more than half a million, and that was just in the last month. Four simultaneous suicide bombing attacks were reported in France and the numbers of the dead are not yet known. Three hurricanes building up strength over different parts of the Atlantic, are all converging into one huge storm on a trajectory to hit the eastern seaboard of the United States in the next 72 hours. Two volcanoes suddenly erupted overnight; Koryaksky in Russia's far east peninsula and Planchon-Peteroa along the border of Chile and Argentina. Scientists are still observing. An earthquake shook Indonesia measuring 8.0 on the Richter scale overnight, hundreds died. The earthquake triggered a Tsunami warning. The impact will not be known for several hours.

"Hmmm", I think to myself. "5-4-3-2-1. Sounds like a countdown." I reach over to turn off the radio and pray grimly, "Lord, the Spirit and the Bride say 'Come!'"

News like that first thing in the morning could set the tone for a really bad day. As much as I hate the clanging of alarm clocks, it must be better than catastrophic news filling the airwaves hourly. Every single headline is crammed with calamitous facts that would have been unfathomable even one year ago. I reset the alarm.

The recent disasters and resulting horror that has occurred almost daily, causes me to begin my days with prayer and journaling. The Earth is getting closer to the end. All over the world there is less and less freedom to speak, worship and live life. There are curfews and a military presence in the streets to enforce them. Information obtained through computer searches, private emails and online purchases are stored in a central database and used against those who foolishly believe they have a right to privacy. Some have willingly given up privacy in exchange for security from terrorism, though even private citizens are accused of being terrorists now.

People are interrogated for their beliefs and some have disappeared altogether—even in the United States, the land of the free and home of the brave. People have taken liberties with the earth, inadvertently causing ecological disasters trying to save the planet. Food is getting scarce all over the earth. Capitalism has been eliminated in most of the world and been replaced with socialism at best and communism at worst. Protestors meet with the harshest of punishment; examples must be made, and precedents set.

I take my hot, strong coffee to my favorite chair in the living room and instantly feel the presence of the Lord waiting for me. We have a standing appointment to talk every morning. I pick up my pen and begin to write, "Good morning, Adonai." He hears a few sentences of mine and then I ask Him what He would like to say to me. This morning He says:

"The time is coming soon. Do not get lost in today for tomorrow things will change dramatically. Do not make the victories of today your be-all and end-all. Your success, and what comes with it, cannot be the idol that keeps your feet stuck in concrete. Look toward the eternal, for your eternity has already begun. See things from an eternal perspective. With whom will you share eternity? Who will look into your eyes in the eternity of eternities with gratitude that you were bold, that your heart overflowed with compassion and that you were obedient to the Word of God in your heart and mind? I AM faithful and true. Let men see your good works and give Me glory for them. Honor Me. Praise Me. Pray that My Kingdom will be on Earth and My will be done in your sphere of authority.

The day is soon coming, when the masses will fall down and worship the one whose souls he hates, the offspring of Satan. He will glory in their adoration and the blood of the saints will pool around his ankles. Finally, nothing will hold him back. And the bowls of Revelation will be poured out on the earth. That time is nearly here. It will be short in elapsed time but wide in scope. Much destruction will be wrought.

Until that day, love and speak to those I bring before you. I will give you courage. I will give you the words. Don't waste a single opportunity."

I re-read my journal entry and think, "There cannot be much time left."

As I finish getting dressed for work, I glance into the bathroom mirror to put the finishing touches on my hair and makeup. The face that stares back at me is intelligent and reasonably pretty. My eyes are hazel, my lips are full, my cheekbones are high, and my nose is turned up slightly at the end. I brush through my dark brown tresses and see two new gray hairs peeking through and, resisting the urge to yank them out, I turn to the full-length mirror. I look objectively at my reflection, thinking that I continue to look younger than my 44 years of age

Its already 7:33 in the morning and I am running late for work. I turn to kiss my husband, Joshua. It is hard to believe we have been married twenty years already. I close the door behind me and hurry off to work.

My name is Isabella Krieger and I work in sales for a small gourmet foods and cookware company located in Chicago, Illinois. My role is to take orders for the products we sell, and I enjoy it. Lately, however, I feel as though I am cemented to the desk chair in my office. I would like to be out with the people face-to-face, flying from place-to-place, and seeing the places and nations from which our products come.

I received a prophetic word several years ago saying that I would set my feet on all seven continents and pray for the nations within them. With the governments of the world aligning with the leadership of the United Nations, freedom to travel, especially to share the Gospel, will soon be a challenge. The Lord has told me repeatedly that marketplace ministry can happen wherever I am, reminding me to be patient, to wait on Him. I am working to rid myself of my inclination to grumble and complain and to have gratitude in all things.

As I drive to work, I see the darkness in the atmosphere. The effects of terrorism and suicide bombers worldwide are visible here, especially in front of skyscrapers and government buildings. The streets are getting narrower as cement blockades consume valuable real estate. Cameras are bolted to telephone poles, apartment buildings, stoplights and street signs. Privacy is rapidly becoming a thing of the past as we give it up for the illusive concept of security. Billboards and the sides of buses advertise sex and every pleasure known to man. I pass by evidence of poverty and crime every day—prostitutes, drunks, and the same man asleep in a doorway. "Lord, send laborers into their path. Let them know You and make You Lord over their lives. Let them spend eternity with You, Lord."

My workday is productive. I am the funny and witty one at the office. I am a Christ follower but there is nothing dry or boring, gullible or stupid about me. My cohorts come to me, sometimes in secret, when their spirits are down or when they are irritable, and I lift them up. There is a light in me and most of them know Who that is, whether we talk about Him or not. Some have come to me for prayer when they or their loved ones are sick.

I am able to have a little contact with the people from the company who are responsible for the development and manufacture of our private label of pots, pans, and professional chef knives. They have an office in Romania and the Lord has told me to pray for them all by name. Of the twelve that work there, I have met only two in person, but the Lord has targets of love on all their backs. I know they are part of the reason why this is the position I have.

As my workday ends, I start for home, seeing different faces but with the same ravages of the times in which we live. Deep darkness covers the people and the Lord reminds me that I am the light because He is the Light. I am in Him and He is in me. I turn into the parking lot of the grocery store intending to pick up something to grill for dinner. It is early in the month of August and it has been a hot day, but instead of a bright and sunny late afternoon sun, the sky is dark and there is a chill in the air. I can hear muted traffic sounds miles away, but everything here is completely silent, not even the tweet of a bird, the squeak of a bicycle tire, or the bounce of a basketball at a nearby park. There is no peace in the silence. It is like being in a sound-proof room where every thud, whisper, note or vibration is suffocated; absorbed by a wet blanket.

Odd. The parking lot is nearly empty. So are both the main and side streets that border the store. It's rush hour and there is no traffic at all. There should be people and cars everywhere. The whole block looks like a movie set where a terrible evil is about to happen. There is only one car parked near the entrance and something tells me not to park near it. I feel the hair on the back of my neck rise as I pull my car into a parking spot near the street exit. I ignore the warning in my spirit and get out of the car, turning to grab my purse from the passenger seat.

I am halfway across the parking lot when suddenly a massive black SUV comes from nowhere, barreling over the curb heading straight for me. The windows are tinted black and I cannot see the driver. Puzzlement turns to terror as I realize that this is no accident. Time seems to stop, as I comprehend that the scene has been staged, waiting for my arrival. There is no place to run and no obstacle to hide behind as I hear the car accelerating. The last thing I hear is my own scream cut off as I am run down. I feel searing pain and then everything goes black.

In spite of the violent attack on me, all remains quiet. There is no sound of traffic, automobile, commuter train or airplane, no human voice or the bark of a dog. After a few minutes, my spirit leaves my body on the cracked asphalt parking lot, still warm from the searing August heat. My spirit is ascending, rising slowly, higher and higher, inches at a time. I can see myself lying on the ground below me as I rise to meet my God. My corpse is twisted and bleeding, a large gash visible on my forehead, across the bridge of my nose and my mouth as I have nearly bit through my tongue.

I see the door of the grocery store open and a single young grocery store stocker exits the building and walks slowly toward me. He is about 35 years old, slipping the apron off over his head. His hair is jet black and his complexion is so pale he is nearly translucent blue. He looks like a premature infant, the veins visible on his forehead. He is not running. His gait isn't urgent. He is attentive but his expression is almost bored. He takes a cigarette out of his shirt pocket and begins to light it when suddenly a fifteen-foot angel, wings fully extended, lands with a loud swish between my body and the young man. He looks up as terrified as I was just a few minutes ago and turns to run.

The angel is dressed in full body armor and chain mail. He holds a five-foot sword in his right hand and a huge oval shield in his left. Covering his head is a helmet also made of chain mail. He is massive and I cannot help but feel that he is ancient, having been in existence for eons.

All of a sudden, I hear a whoosh of air and then a thump and realize that I am back in my body and in excruciating pain. There is not a single square inch of flesh that isn't screaming in agony. I try to move but nothing is working. I can't move. I can't breathe. I am having difficulty seeing. My pelvis is fractured, my ribs broken, my lungs collapsed. In my abdomen there is internal bleeding, my left knee is crushed, and I have compound fractures in both tibias and fibulas. I feel like death and am not sure why my exit from the earth realm to the heavenly one was abruptly reversed.

The angel allows the young man to run. The Lord will deal with him in His time. He turns to look down at me, his expression intense and angry but there is compassion in his gray eyes. He lays his right hand on my forehead above the gash and with his left he quickly but gently takes my hand. He lifts his eyes to the sky and begins to speak in a language I have never heard before. He cries out to Heaven as if he feels all of my intense suffering. The pain leaves me abruptly and I am suddenly and completely healed! Every fractured bone put back into perfect alignment, my lungs fully expanding, every wound made whole. I sit up, gingerly touching all the areas that were in agony just seconds ago, but everything is restored to normal except for a one-inch red scratch on my forehead where the deep gash had been.

I look hard at the angel and wait for an explanation. Who tried to kill me and why? Who is the angel and how did he happen upon me as I lay dying? How did they control the traffic … and who are *they*? How will I explain my appearance to my husband? Is there a fight between good and evil over me as the appearance of an angel would indicate and if so, why today of all days?

All of a sudden, the angel shrinks from fifteen feet tall to six feet and his wings become invisible. He is no longer clothed in armor with sword in hand. He is now wearing jeans and a black T-shirt. His hair is sandy-colored, cut short, and his eyes are dark gray. He is handsome in his way, but his eyes are serious and sincere, and it is obvious he is on a mission.

He tells me in all seriousness, "There has been an assignment against you for millions of years."

I look at him agreeing that there was definitely an assignment against me tonight but trying not to laugh at the statement he has just made. If I laugh now, I will be unable to control the hysteria that is quickly rising in me.

I respond with a shaky smile. "I must be pretty important to have any assignment, good or evil, for millions of years."

The angel says, "My name is Trent and I have been assigned to you since your birth. You have a very important assignment and it's about to begin. It was planned before the world was even created. Satan, the Devil formerly known as Lucifer, gave orders to his minions to take you out so that you cannot fulfill it. He has demons and humans all over the earth ready to do his bidding. Your mission will begin in the next few days and you will be protected until it is completed. I was attacked in the air trying to get to you today and have called forth a legion to protect you from this point forward."

He continued, "Drive home now and stay inside. You will have hundreds of angels, some seen and most not, to ensure that you are safe and secure until you can execute the orders that you are given. I am always with you. Know that you are never alone."

Trent walks me back to my car and sees me safely inside, seat belt fastened. As I start the car I look up into the sky, startled to see black clouds on the horizon. These are not storm clouds, but I don't know what to compare them to, as I've never seen anything like them before. They are almost seaweed green and twisted, layer upon layer. They are as organized as an army and their presence startles me, especially after the events of the past hour. As I pull out of the parking lot, they are in my rearview mirror and I keep my eye on them, not exactly sure what I expect them to do if I look away.

As I drive home, the shock of the violent hit and run rushes to my memory and my hands begin to shake. I hear a voice in my spirit that reminds me that God will never leave me nor forsake me and peace floods over me. As I pull my car into the garage, Joshua greets me and asks where I've been. It is later than usual. His eyes are worried, and it is as if he could feel in the atmosphere the trouble I've had tonight.

I remember the angel Trent's, words about an important assignment in the near future. I discern easily that it is an assignment from God, and I don't want Joshua to come against it because he is afraid for me. I deliberately lighten my tone and say, "I stopped at the grocery store to pick up something for dinner but decided to crash here at home instead. Want to order a pizza?"

Later, as I turn out the light, I realize just how tired I am. I need to get to sleep so I can get up tomorrow and do it all again (with the exception of the murder attempt, of course). I snuggle close to Joshua and my eyes close.

CHAPTER 3
THE EVENING
ON THE MOUNTAIN

DAY 1, TUESDAY, AUGUST 11, 12:03 A.M.–T MINUS 39
ISABELLA KRIEGER

Though I fell asleep the instant my head touched the pillow, I am awakened within ten minutes, fully alert. The alarm clock next to my bed blinks 12:03 a.m., bright red in the darkness. I sit straight up in my bed, wondering what has awakened me, when I feel the atmosphere change, rippling with an electric charge. Suddenly a large portal opens in the ceiling above my bed and I am pulled through it at the speed of light. The brightness of the portal is so intense I have to close my eyes and still it shines in. It is as though darkness and light are clashing swords all around me, but strangely I feel no fear at all, only great expectation. It's as if I had waited all my life for this moment.

A few seconds later, I find myself on a beautiful but very stark mountaintop. The sky is gun metal gray in the early morning light, dark clouds roll on the horizon far below and the only visible colors are dark blue and pale purple heather covering the rocky ground.

I gaze at my surroundings. I see about 150 people of all ages and races. There are children as young as three years old, men and women in their ninth decade and every age in between. The very young ones are accompanied by their angels and show no fear, their eyes filled with wisdom. We are from nations all over the world and few of us have language in common.

Though we are comprised of the full spectrum of ages, each one has kind eyes filled with wisdom, and the faith and wonder of a child. Within seconds we are transformed. Each of us stands tall—physically, emotionally and mentally as healthy and fit 33-year-old adults. We are all identically dressed in silver chain mail armor from head to foot.

Suddenly a tall angel appears in our midst, but we are not confused about his origin. He is dressed as we are, nearly twelve feet tall with a wingspan of twenty feet. His wings are the color of beautiful ivory that shines bright even in the dull light, and the pinions look like fine gold. His eyes are like fire, his expression grim even as he welcomes us as brothers and sisters in arms. In his right hand is a scroll, which he unrolls. It is a word from the Lord. The angel begins to read aloud in a language none of us have ever heard but each of us understands.

"Before you were born, I knew you. Long before the foundation of the world, I called you. As assignments were given and times and places decided, the End of Days Special Forces were determined. I asked all of creation, billions of people over the course of time, 'Who will go?' Each of you, 144 in number, answered quickly, 'Send me.' You are a remnant within a remnant, representing every nation, tribe, and tongue.

Picture the prophet Joel's Valley of Decision as if it were the Red Sea parting for the Israelites to walk on dry ground. On the left and right are the waters that have been parted and the middle is dry ... empty. In the Valley of Decision, the valley still contains millions of people who don't know their options, even at this late date in time, or are not sure which side of the fence they are on. On one side are those that are for Me and on the other are those that are for anything else. Even with the billion souls brought in through stadium revivals over the last eighteen months, many remain in the valley and many more throughout history who were missed.

The worlds are at war and have been since the dawning of time. The spiritual and natural worlds are in a battle over My creation. Time is coming to an end and there is much to be done. I AM taking your face in My hands to remind you of promises you made before the foundation of the Earth. It is now time to fulfill them. Today, and for the next forty days, each of your destinies will be fully realized."

I think of the angel Trent and his words over me just a few short hours ago. This is the mission and the reason for Lucifer's hatred of me for millions of years. He hates each one of us. For all the time that the world has existed, the enemy has known his time is brief and very rapidly fleeting. He is in panic mode and that makes him very dangerous indeed.

The angel stands straight at attention, then bends down on one knee, and bows his head in absolute reverence. Startled, each of us turns to see what has captured his attention. There, behind us, is the King of all kings, dressed in a white linen garment with a golden sash and a magnificent many-jeweled crown upon His head. His eyes are as blazing fire and His hair as white as wool. The spicy fragrance of balsam and frankincense fill the air. When He speaks, His voice is more beautiful than any I have ever heard, authoritative, yet smooth as honey.

"I gave My life for the people of the Earth and I still fight for them, interceding day and night before My Father. If you only knew how much I love those who are Mine. When I walked on the Earth, those My Father gave Me were guarded and protected, not one of them lost, except the son of perdition.

You have not been mistakenly chosen for this assignment. I knew exactly what I was doing when I chose you.

I see the end from the beginning. Some of those that are Mine have been deceived and have succumbed to the enemy's attacks. Some became so weary they could not go on and missed their destiny, affecting the lives of others who would be Mine. Others allowed circumstances to dictate truth to them and their feet became mired in cement, stuck in time and unable to move forward. Still others have not yet heard about Me and My glorious Kingdom. Not one of those destined for eternity with Me will be lost, even if it appears in the present, and from the past, as if it is too late. Not even one.

Your assignment: Retrieve them."

Each of us, one by one is called up by name to the short platform from which the angel has spoken. We kneel on one knee as I imagine Gideon once did when he was called a mighty man of valor and received his commission to lead the Israelites to victory over the Midianite army. With head bowed, the Sword of the Spirit—Jesus—lays His own sword of Wisdom, Understanding, Counsel and Might, Revelation and the Reverential Fear of His Father on both shoulders and atop the head of each of this small remnant. He imparts wisdom that exceeds that of Solomon, boldness that exceeds that of Paul, and favor that exceeds that of Joseph. Each of us is given a magnificent shield and a five-foot sword to be used in every mission—a sword that could be used as a dagger of five inches in length, or one that could span the length of a room, along with the physical strength and ability to use it victoriously.

All at once the scene shifts and we all see from a different perspective. The light that had been on us from above now moves from the ground up. The top of the mountain on which we stand becomes the floor of a giant Coliseum. We are standing in the center, surrounded by theater seating. In the seats on the main floor and in balconies that appear as if suspended from Heaven, are legions of angels and they are also wearing armor and carrying shields and swords. In the first balcony there are hundreds of angels wearing white robes with silver sashes. In the second, third and fourth balconies there are thousands of people, old and young, many with tears falling down their cheeks and joy in their eyes. These are the Great Cloud of Witnesses. They are those who have lived on the earth and fulfilled the calling on their lives in their lifetime and have gone to Heaven ahead of us.

It is so quiet that all could hear the sound of a pin dropping as Jesus continued.

"The world as it is will go through much hardship as the Great Tribulation begins. You are warriors to the nations. Your mandate is to retrieve those who would be Mine and leave none behind."

The sound in the open air is deafening as Angels and Witnesses cheer and shout. Many have waited millennia upon millennia for this moment. They are not only cheering for this moment in time but for each of us as if they were spectators to the race that only we can run.

CHAPTER 4
THE WORDS OF THE ANGEL

LATER THE SAME DAY
ISABELLA KRIEGER

Suddenly, I am awakened and the alarm on my clock is clanging, 6:00 a.m.

I turn off the alarm and lie back in my bed, wondering if the night on the mountain with my Lord and the angel had been a wild dream. I have no recollection of returning to my bed and have no idea how I got here or when. The angel's words reverberate in my mind, over and over like echoes of sounds on mountaintops or in caves. Like a special frequency that only I can hear, the words are both seen and heard. Though I know they are from the Book of Isaiah and that I have read them many times, the words I recognize are for me alone.

"I asked all of creation, billions of people over the course of time, 'who will go' and each of you, 144 in number, answered quickly, 'send me.' You are a remnant within a remnant, representing every nation, tribe, and tongue."

The Lord whispers into my mind, reminding me that He had chosen me before time began to be an intermittent encourager to the others, to remind them of the seriousness of their commitment so long ago. I am the witness to the gathering of every star, every human being who would ever live on the Earth, billions of them, and many angels, too, held in Heaven so long ago. My thoughts are filled with the memory of the sights, sounds and fragrances of Heaven before time began. The Lord continues to speak, telling me I am to be the scribe for what will take place over the next forty days. The words that are written will be read from a scroll at the marriage supper of the Lamb. The memories have come flooding back. He had asked all of the stars, *"Who will go for us"* before the world was created, before we had a physical body, a name, or a specific timeframe on the Earth, and I remembered the responses of the 144 of us. We agreed with God and all of Heaven to participate in the mission of the last days Special Forces of Light, codenamed Light Ops.

The words of the angel came rushing back as he gave us instructions on the mission, our weapons, threats to completion, and tools of communication. Though there are 144 of us from every nation, tribe, and tongue, our nations of origin would not dictate the location of our assignments. As there are missionaries from Africa ministering to people in the United States or Germans in China, so, too, would we as a team, cross all borders. We would be equipped for every mission including innate knowledge of foreign languages. God's thoughts are higher than ours and His reasons would prevail.

We represent all age groups on Earth—from three to eighty-four years old. When we perform our daily assignments, we will be our "heavenly age" of thirty-three years—the age Jesus was victorious over death and the grave. In most cases we would be alone except for the team of angels assigned to accompany each of us. In some cases, we would be assigned with another, a partner for that day's mission. On at least three occasions, there would be ten or more of us in a territory, working toward the same end. But, we would start out miles apart and probably would not see each other with our physical eyes.

Time would be stretched, and distance compressed. At any point in each of the forty days, we would be deployed. Most often it would be while we slept at night, as it was last night. Other times, we would walk through a natural doorway and instantly arrive in a destination across the world. Some would close their eyes in prayer and instantaneously arrive in the nation they had prayed for only seconds before.

Missions would be secret—covert, as we attempt to stay hidden from the forces of darkness. This would be short lived however, as the forces of darkness would soon be able to discern the Light, much as we made it a practice to determine whether darkness or light were rulers in a region.

Our mission was not to rescue the lost in order that they might live long on Earth, but to grow the Kingdom of God and save those who would otherwise be eternally lost. Relationships would be forged; multi-generational children who had never been born, would be. They would teach their children about Jesus, the King of kings and Lord of lords; ancestors whose destinies had been overturned by the Devil would be restored. Resources would be made available and multitudes saved. People would be able to touch the lives of others when it could not have been accomplished had they never been born.

Sometimes the redemption would be immediate but more often than not, it would occur over time from then until now. Entire families that do not exist today because of a sin, a demonic attack, a death, or a poorly chosen life path in the past, would be redeemed and in existence when we returned to our present life. History will have already been re-written. There would be no "before" and "after" to document the effects of our activities. We could look at a historical account today of a path taken decades, centuries, or even millennia ago, all because of our assignments to redeem the lost and change that path. Everything would have been changed by our return, as if the reason for which we had been sent had never happened.

The new history books would reveal only the effects of our having been there, family-by-family, city-by-city, and nation-by-nation. The only documentation that would exist would be the Book of Deeds that I had been tasked to write. It is a book of remembrance of these forty days and a recording of our Light Ops team activities for the vast archives of Heaven.

Traveling across the world and across time, our activities might be for one person's redemption or for the redemption of millions. The greater numbers would be accomplished within China, India, and the Middle East. We would go where no other believer had ever traveled over the course of time. As Phillip was translated to minister to the Ethiopian, so too, would we be translated through time and space to our assigned places and people groups, redeeming individuals, families, villages, cities and nations. And it would all occur in forty days.

The angel stepped to his right and another angel, who had been standing behind him, stepped forward. He had been introduced as Bennett, the Strategy and Communications Officer of Heaven. He was about eight feet tall and had a wingspan of six feet. He would be the point person for the Light Ops Special Forces, directing both humans and the heavenly host in our missions. He wore round wire-rimmed glasses and had a cherubic face, blue eyes and slightly rosy cheeks. He saluted us and, with a trace of tears in his eyes, told us that all of Heaven would rejoice at all the lost souls we brought in before it was too late.

At this point, the angel could discern questions about this approach of God's to redeem those that were already lost. The angel was not angry or disturbed at the questions. They were not born in doubt or unbelief. He had been present when Mary was given her choice to be the virgin mother of the Lord Jesus Christ. He had been the one to answer her question, "How can this be, seeing I have not known a man?" Her question was asked to gain understanding and not questioning the Source in unbelief. Likewise, the questions in the minds of some of the warriors had to do with why God would not ensure that people were protected. Why did He not intervene to ensure all babies were born and make sure all decisions regarding path of life were guaranteed to be in line with God's plans? Why hadn't appointments and relationships been divinely arranged in time? Why go in after the fact?

The angel's answers were simple and direct. "Jesus, the Lamb of God was slain before the foundation of the Earth. He knew Adam and Eve would fall. He was not shocked by it. It did not take Him by surprise. He did not have to scramble to correct the problem and He didn't "fix it" before it occurred. He wasn't worried. And He did not destroy Adam and Eve and start humankind over again, as was His prerogative.

Likewise, when the Israelites had sinned, Jesus did not destroy the entire world. Moses intervened and relied on the nature and character of God to preserve His creation. And again, when the bloodlines of mankind were corrupted and evil was rampant on the Earth, the destiny of mankind was preserved through the bloodline of Noah and his sons, even as the rest of the living were destroyed in the flood. God sees all and He has already seen all, from beginning to end. He sees the end from the beginning, as a complete timeline. Provisions had been made before Earth was created.

You were the solution, by your own agreement, before time began, to play a large role in bringing the fullness of the Gentiles into the Kingdom of God. When all is accomplished, the Earth will change dramatically. The Body of Christ, each cell a living, breathing follower of Jesus, with Him as the Head, will leave this Earth leaving behind those without a relationship with the three persons of God: Father, Son and Holy Spirit. Only the Jewish race, the 144,000 virgins, 12,000 from each of the twelve tribes to evangelize the nation of Israel, and the lost, will remain on the Earth. Evil will fill the Earth; Demons scrambling up through manhole covers and deep fissures in the ground with no believer in sight to rebuke and take authority over them. You can already discern that the cup is nearly full."

I realized as I remembered the encounter with Jesus and the angel on the mountaintop, that I was not merely thinking about it but was able to hear their voices. It was as if the words were transcribed in light behind my eyes. The angel had explained that no matter where we were, or at which point in time, we would never be alone. We would never have any questions about the assignment, the target, the mission, the tools we needed to accomplish it, or the impact. We would know who would be saved, how many, and "ripples in the pool" from our activities. We would not fail.

The angel went on and said that, just like our "regular" lives, the sin we allowed in our hearts would make our walk much more difficult. The enemy could come in through a crack that sin would create in our armor. So, we needed to stay out of pride, fear, unforgiveness, and bitterness. Our assignments could be accomplished with ease, or each task could be done as if running through quicksand, where every battle with demonic strongholds would take every ounce of our strength. We should keep ourselves strong by praying in the Spirit and taking communion at least daily, not as an empty ritual but as a remembrance of our own redemption. Forgiving others and repentance would be paramount to our timely success. Those of us who were "backslidden" would make their peace with God and end up strong in the Lord and the power of His might. Doing any of these missions in our own strength would be nearly impossible.

I move to rise, and I realize that I have new energy in my body. Every ache and pain that I had come to know as a part of aging, is now gone! I feel as energetic as a fifteen-year-old, clearheaded and fully awake. I splash water on my face and brush my teeth in an attempt to get to work before the heat of the day intensifies. As I see my reflection in the mirror, I gasp in surprise. My hair has a streak of platinum in my normally auburn-colored hair on the right side of my face. As the face of Moses shone with the glory of the Lord on Mount Sinai, His glory is now resting in my hair. I wonder with joy how many other changes I will see in myself and how in the world I will explain them.

My living room chair waits for me as I sit to wait on the Lord. As excited as I am about my new assignment and about my encounter with the Lord, I must quiet myself to hear Him. My journal entry from the Lord today is an awesome one, as always:

"Boldness in your marketplace activities will be as nothing as you answer My call to destiny. You will be equipped with what you need to accomplish it.

A remnant is a small subcategory of a larger group. The Body of Christ is a remnant of all those living on the earth right now. The Light Ops Special Forces are a remnant of the Body of Christ, a very specialized group indeed. Though you are operating in secret, your activities and those of My "remnant within a remnant" will be known throughout the current and future Church in the land of the living.

I will be getting you up in the night season to accomplish what is needed and will equip you during the day to walk and work with energy, vigor, and creativity. You will spend much time with a Mona Lisa smile on your face. I can pull the past into the present and interject you far into the future.

People need to have fear removed and walk in hope. They need to have a view of Me rarely seen because of the deception of the enemy who blames Me for every negative thing that has happened over the course of time.

I am calling those not yet in My sheepfold and talking to those who do not yet recognize My voice. I want them to know Me, to understand that I AM the Captain of the host. I am calling them to understand the concept of redemption: redeeming sin, making it as though it had never happened, redeeming time so that it is never too late, and in the process, truly restoring hope.

It is time to capture the hearts of those who will be Mine. You are protected. My angels fight alongside you, harkening to My words flowing from your lips. You wear new armor and a new mantle never worn before. You are not alone. Like Elijah, when he ran from evil Jezebel, there were 7,000 who had not eaten food sacrificed to idols. You are not alone.

Walk in joy and hope today. Those who wait on me will gain new strength. You have never before had such energy, vigor, and strength, victorious one. You will mount up on My wings. You will walk, run, and fly, getting stronger and leaner with every moment. Agree with Me. I will fill you with Light that cannot be extinguished. Do not get distracted. Rely on Me alone."

I begin to pray while I get myself ready for work. "Lord, let me be a living epistle today, keep me pure in word, thought and deed … "

CHAPTER 5
THE LIBRARY OF HEAVEN

SAME DAY, AT 10:41 P.M.
ISABELLA KRIEGER
CHICAGO, IL

Tonight, like last night, I have been asleep for only minutes when suddenly I am awakened by the sound of the portal opening over my bed. I glance over at Joshua who is sound asleep, and I have to wonder if only I can hear this incredible noise. It sounds like a huge manhole cover sliding off the mammoth space it conceals. Can he not see the extreme light? Is his sleep supernaturally deep? My eyes return to the portal in my ceiling and I am suddenly sucked head-first into it at warp speed.

I can hear the sounds of swords clashing, louder than the first time and I realize I am passing through the heavens. First out of Earth's atmosphere, entering the Second Heaven—AKA "Outer Space", then on my way to the third Heaven. The Second Heaven represents the high places referred to in Ephesians 6, the area where principalities and powers and the rulers of darkness of this world and spiritual wickedness in high places hold court to strategize and execute their plans against mankind. Every motive is to harass, intimidate, create chaos, deceive, kill and destroy them. Angelic forces, deployed from the Third Heaven, are fighting our battles in answer to the prayers of the saints. The battle sounds are vicious, and I can hear the cries of demons as they are put down.

Within seconds, I am in the Library of Heaven. All around me are fifty-foot tall shelves reaching from the floor to the very high ceiling. They are filled with books, from tiny ones the size of an American dime, to huge scholarly tomes. On one wall there is a massive stone fireplace, the blaze glowing golden orange. The air smells of wood smoke and old books. In the center of the vast room is a wide wooden table made from one of the oldest substances on earth, kauri wood in the color of warm cognac. On it are six ancient books: The Book of Bodily Members, The Book of the Wars of the Lord (YHWH's Battles), the complete Holy Bible, The Book of Remembrance, The Book of Deeds and most important, The Book of Life. I am seated at a long mahogany table in a comfortably padded, upright chair. The chair is a beautiful shade of mixed gold and silver I have never seen before. All around me angels are putting books on shelves, high on ladders, pushing carts, and whispering to others to please be quiet.

Jesus Himself strides in and I fall on my face in awe. The atmosphere changes and I become breathless in His presence. The fragrance of pine, frankincense and warm spice surround Him, and I want to breathe deep and bury my head in His neck. He puts His hand lightly on top of my head and murmurs words in a language I have never heard before and then tells me to sit back down. He needs to remind me of where we are in time to make sure I understand the urgency of our mission and my part to communicate it to the others. He sits down at the head of the long library table and Bennett sits across from me. He looks at me in all seriousness.

"No man knows the hour of My return. It will be as a thief in the night, the blink of an eye and at a time no one expects. Wise men know the season and many of the signs have now come to pass. Prophesies in both the Old and New Testaments are already fulfilled, but there are still some that have yet to come to pass. Specifically, those in Ezekiel, Daniel, and Revelation. There continue to be wars and rumors of wars, but there is one coming soon that I alone will win. My victory will be the trigger for both the Rapture of My Body of believers—the Ekklesia, and the Great Tribulation. No longer will there be a valley of decision. If a person has not chosen to follow Me, their decision has been made by default and they will remain on the earth for the Tribulation. Therefore, no decision made is a decision made. They can still be saved as there will be many who knew of Me but without a relationship with Me. They will be brought home at the End of the Age, if they have not received the Mark of the Beast or recanted their faith, having endured the "wrath to come".

You have heard the phrase 'as in the days of Noah' and you are indeed in them now. Great evil is in the earth, more than ever before, but Noah lived in an especially evil time as well. Then the Nephilim reigned, angels intermarrying with the daughters of men and creating a no-longer-human race; violent, murderous and chaotic. Those on Earth didn't give it a thought, so involved were they in their own pleasures, marrying and giving in marriage. They were so desensitized that evil had become mundane. It is the same now in your time.

"Let's talk about Ezekiel's War", Jesus continues. *"As I know you know, the war I am talking about can be found in Ezekiel 38 and 39."*

I quickly run to the table of tomes and bring the huge Holy Bible back to my chair, open it to Book of Ezekiel and begin to read as He expounds on this topic and creates an urgency in Me that I have never felt before. People need to be told where they are in time. There is very little of it left.

The spiritual storm clouds are gathering green-black and roiling on the horizon. Schemes and plans being made in the war rooms of goat nations, those nations that hate Israel and hate Me, and tactics for war are being established. Like a tornado coming in minutes on the movies you watch, there is little time left to bring people to safety. It is time to gather the remnant into the storm shelter. When the storm arrives, they will be safe, and the door will be closed. I, the Bridegroom, will shut the door.

All that has been prophesied will come to pass.

Once again, it is imperative that My Special Forces of Light recognize the urgency of this 40-day Mission. All who are seeking after Me have recognized the season for decades, perhaps even one hundred years. My Forces must be able to see the dark clouds gathering on the horizon and discern that the time is near. Every person and nation that belongs to Me must be gathered in before I shut the door.

The nations are My inheritance and at the end of the age, every knee will bow, and every tongue confess that I AM Lord."

Again, I hear verses of scripture in my spirit that I speak out loud. *"The kingdom of the world has become the Kingdom of our God and of His Anointed One. He will reign supreme for an eternity of eternities!"*[10]

Jesus says, *"There are people praying all over the world for the kingdoms of this world to come in on bended knee to Me. Look over and see."*

I look over at the wall that He has pointed to and a six-foot monitor is rising up out of the floor showing multiple screens of people, one at a time, two in agreement, prayer groups in homes and in revivals in stadiums. All over the world I can hear a cacophony of voices in many languages naming the nations, one at a time.

One group calls out, *"Kyrgyzstan, Laos, Latvia, Lebanon, Lesotho, Liberia, Libya, Liechtenstein, Lithuania, Luxembourg, Macau, Macedonia … "*

"Rumänien, Russland, Ruanda, Saudi-Arabien, Senegal, Serbien und Montenegro, Seychellen, Sierra Leone, Slowakei … " another calls out in German.

Other voices continue in French, *"Ouganda, Ukraine, Émirats arabes unis, Royaume-Uni, États-Unis, Uruguay, Ouzbékistan … "*

And in Argentinian Spanish more nations are spoken in intercession, *"Japón, Jordania, Kazajstán, Kenia, Kiribati, Corea del Norte y del Sur … "*

A single woman's voice murmurs from a rocking chair as she knits, *"Australia, Austria, Azerbaijan, Bahrain, Bangladesh, Belarus, Belgium … "*

"I charge you, Isabella, to be a voice in the ears of the other Forces of Light, much like they will hear Bennett instruct them. You will entreat them, remind them of the gathering storm, and work to get all of Mine to safety. The fullness of time has nearly arrived."

CHAPTER 6

Z-BAR, TZ, EAST AFRICA

DAY 2, WEDNESDAY, AUGUST 12 – T MINUS 38
PRISCILLA GRAHAM
LONDON, ENGLAND

Isabella, from the Library of Heaven, describes the qualities and history of Patricia Graham, the warrior she is observing:

Priscilla Graham is a picture of a Deborah. She is strong in the Lord and has been all her life. Not one of her experiences has been wasted, whether pleasant or painful, as her accumulated knowledge expands her wisdom. Though I have only met her two days ago, she is a favorite of mine in the Special Forces of Light.

Priscilla Graham comes from a short list of saints, but the Lord has fully equipped her for her forty-day assignment. He has performed a quick work in her.

Priscilla is sixty-eight years old, a secondary school teacher all her adult life who retired three years ago. She was born and raised in Auckland, Australia. She was married to Jim Graham, her husband of forty-three years and widowed within a year of retirement. They were together from high school through college, married immediately after graduation, taught in the same high school and retired the same day. They had no children, a source of pain for them both, but transferred their need to love their own children to the teenagers at the school where they both taught. They celebrated victories together, suffered loss together and were each other's right arm. A month after they retired, Jim was diagnosed with advanced lung cancer and was gone nine months later. Priscilla has been devastated but the Lord has always been her strength. The most difficult part of the last two years has been a sense of having no purpose in life.

Two days ago, Priscilla was given her marching orders and every morning since, she has been eager to rise. Her own destiny is intertwined with those of the Light Ops Forces and those they have come to redeem.

PRISCILLA:

Coming to church today has a whole new meaning since meeting the Lord face-to-face, witnessing His majesty and eyes filled with fiery love. I can see Him, not merely imagine His face. I have come to fellowship with those around me but more than that, to worship with all of myself—spirit, soul, and body. I sing my praises and I dance in worship as all our voices lift as one.

As we sit to hear the message, I am struck suddenly with an urge to pray for protection for the believers in East Africa and for the Muslims to come into the Kingdom of God. I find myself visualizing the island of Zanzibar on the east coast of Tanzania, a place I have visited before "in the natural". I close my eyes to pray for the beautiful people in Zanzibar and begin to feel a warm breeze on my face. I hear voices as people pass me and realize that they are speaking Swahili and that I understand it perfectly.

I open my eyes and find myself in the center of Stone Town, the capital city of Zanzibar. I smell the smokiness that seems to hover over much of Africa, and the sea that is only a few blocks from where I now stand. I am not alone. Next to me are two men, both about six feet tall. One is a sandy-haired man with green eyes and fine freckles on his nose, and the other with almost black hair and blue eyes. Max is the fair-haired one and possesses a soft-spoken voice. Micah has a British accent and a gleam of mischief in his eyes.

Max and Micah will be with me on every mission I have been assigned for the Lord. They have been with me since the day that I was born. They are here to guard and protect me, and I am their "charge" to shield. They are my angels, seen in the flesh.

Max is dressed in a black t-shirt and jeans, and Micah in a gray t-shirt and green cargo pants. Both carry green army fatigue jackets looped through backpacks of the same color. I catch a glimpse of myself in a shopkeeper's window and see that I, too, am dressed in jeans and t-shirt with combat boots on my feet. We could be tourists from any place in the world. What startles me is that my reflection shows me at my heavenly age of 33 instead of my actual 68 years and I find myself grinning in anticipation for the day.

Looking around me, I see many people from Tanzania's mainland and the coastal citizens of Zanzibar milling about. The people of Zanzibar are a mixture in heritage, the impact of all the nations who have traded here over thousands of years, primarily African and Arabic with a strong Portuguese influence that can be seen in the faces and heard in the Swahili language.

Besides the indigenous people and tourists, I see hundreds of angels. I realize they are not visible to the people because there is no response by the humans in the area. The angels are on the street, sitting atop buildings in the square and meeting us from all directions. They each have a mark the color of red henna on their foreheads, as if they are wearing the seal of the King that sent them. As I look to Max and Micah, Max with a twinkle in his eye, pulls his hair off his forehead and there is the same mark; Micah, with the same twinkle, shows me his as well.

One angelic group is watching the skies and wastewater ditches to make sure there is no imminent danger from the demonic hordes that will most certainly fight for their territory. The color of the sky is already beginning to change. Dark blue-brown clouds approach from over the sea, as if a storm is coming.

"There will be a battle here today," I think to myself.

The angels who are watching for trouble are dressed for war. They wear Kevlar and riot gear with a long shining sword at their sides, their faces pure and noble. They are warrior angels, loyal to the death for their Lord and King. But there will be no death here today for those who belong to the Lord ... or those who will.

The other group of angels is comprised of those who are newly assigned to individuals and to the regional territory of Zanzibar. Already they are walking with and among the people. They speak in words not audibly heard by everyone, but rather by whispers in the ears of the people to whom they are assigned. Some of the people change their course, heading in a different direction than they had originally planned to go. Many of those have puzzled expressions on their faces because of it. They are being angelically led, and though the decision to obey is completely their own, they have turned their will to that of the angels.

The Lord is standing in the Situation Room of Heaven and He is watching. His angel, Bennett, is giving me intelligence information, which I can both see and hear as I walk. He directs us to a crossroad just outside the city center where both a mosque and a large Christian church can be seen. This intersection is the Valley of Decision and is strategic for my assignment today. I am not directed to the specific target but am told that I will know him when I see him.

I have traveled nearly 9,000 miles in mid-May of the current year, backward in time, to Zanzibar, a semi-autonomous part of Tanzania, at the end of the month that Ramadan is being observed. The coordinates are: 6°9'57"S and 39°11'57"E. Ninety-seven percent of this island's population of 16,000 is fasting, which is Islam's third pillar, sunrise to sunset, in remembrance of the revelation of the Quran to the prophet Mohammed.

It is now the end of the third of five prayer times that will be held today, and five hundred men depart from the mosque as nearly one hundred others who are guided by the angels converge on the intersection. Max, Micah and I arrive, along with the warrior angels and the ones assigned to assist. Even with all the people within my line of vision, I am astounded at how much sound I can hear. It is a cacophony of noise. I turn my head to find the source of it.

The sounds come from the yard outside the church, which is built on the site of one of Zanzibar's largest slave markets. The altar's location is said to sit on the exact spot of the whipping post, not far from Kilele Square, the site of another slave market. Kilele is the Swahili word for noise. I realize that I am hearing the accumulated noises of hundreds of years. The sounds are deafening to me and transmit the feelings of extreme anxiety and dread. The noise is the sound of the buyers and sellers of men who have been captured throughout the continent of

Africa. It is combined with the anguished cries of men being sold, as their traders beat them into submission.

The sky continues to darken even as the Light of the Gospel moves in. The territorial strongholds over Zanzibar have been strengthening, as less of the light has been allowed to enter. Slavery, torture, murder, and antichrist are the spiritual strongholds over this region and the dark hordes from each of them rush to prevent us from moving forward. As I watch the sky, I can see horrific faces in the clouds. They are forming a circle of thrones over the city of Stone Town, large and small, lining the skies as if they are going to watch a battle of gladiators fighting to the death in an amphitheater.

The spiritual ruler, Slavery sits on a plain, flat wooden chair, very old, very dry and splintered. At the end of the armrests are iron manacles and at the base of the chair legs are two more. The back of the chair is flat and tall, with a metal "headrest" designed to hold a man's head and neck firmly in place. The figure that sits on it is tall, grim and cruel. He is filthy yet fastidious, wearing a black suit and soiled white shirt. He fattens his victims up, not to assuage their hunger but to make them saleable. He treats their disease, not to heal and free them from the threat of death but to receive a return on his investment. He is a businessman with no hint of mercy in him.

Near Slavery sits another spiritual ruler, Torture. He wears black full silk pants with a red cummerbund. He wears no shirt and his muscles ripple. His body is covered in sweat. His head is bald, and he has a thick black mustache. He looks like he belongs in a circus only I can find no amusement in the science of torture. His eyes are small and beady and cruel. His hands are formed like the instruments of torture he uses in his craft. His left hand is a ball peen hammer and his right is comprised of "fingers" which include a drill bit, blade, pliers, and torch. He is a Ruler of Darkness who gives orders to torture but enjoys his role so much that he often executes those orders himself. His throne is a flat wooden bench with a series of short spikes over the entire seat.

The Principality of Murder wears all black—black turtleneck, black jeans, black socks and shoes, black gloves, and black beanie. He is an assassin, a jealous husband, a mobster, and a terrorist. He whispers into the ears of professional killers, "regular" people in a murderous rage, psychopaths and fanatical ideologues and then each has a decision to make; kill or walk away. His eyes are bright blue, alert, furtive, accusing, and coldly frenetic. He is enjoying the activity and he cracks his knuckles in anticipation of joining the fight. His throne is a black leather winged-back armchair, simple, comfortable and not fussy.

The throne for the Principality of Antichrist is the largest and the most ornate, made of pure gold and trimmed in rubies. The chair is bolted atop a pedestal, a massive circle of black onyx, where the Christ-hater elevates himself. The pedestal is the destination of two sets of six stair steps, one on each side of the throne. He is the chief of all of Satan's executives, proud, haughty, arrogant, and enjoying his final role on Earth, which is just beginning. He has walked the Earth many times before, having many names: Nimrod, Nero, Antiochus Epiphanies, Charlemagne, Stalin, and Hitler. He is being readied by Satan to charm and manipulate the world, to put into motion and enforce the Mark of the Beast and to kill and destroy anyone refusing to bow to him and to his father, the Devil.

He turns his head and I see his face. He is handsome with brown eyes and wavy black hair. He is dressed in a black silk suit, a red silk patterned tie, a white kerchief in his suit pocket, and black leather Italian shoes. His grooming is flawless. He is smiling. He looks familiar to me somehow, but I can't fathom why.

Surrounding the thrones are waves of blackened, writhing bodies, groaning in agony and they, too, are watching. It is then that I see the target, the one for whom I was sent. The one who would be the first of thousands from Zanzibar who join the Kingdom of God in this present day. He is a man sitting on the side of the road at the intersection where the religious structures of Zanzibar converge. From the litter around him, and his few belongings, it appears that he spends most of his time here.

The man is about thirty years old, although it is difficult to say because of the harshness of his circumstances. He has no legs. His thighs stop short, directly below his pelvis. His arms look strong and his wrists are hyper-extended. The palms of his hands are large, swollen, and scarred. They are his only form of transportation and function as both hands and feet.

The enemies send in the giants in an attempt to stop me from approaching the man. There are two of them, each thirteen feet tall, completely bald, their heads melting into their shoulders. They are members of the race of Cyclops and their collective eyes are focused on me.

Bennett whispers, "Their names are Idiotis and Moronicus. They are strong, but stupid, and incapable of independent thought. They are slaves to the mighty men of old and they work, day and night, for the food they eat and a horse stable floor to sleep on."

They are dressed in tatters, one carrying a club and the other a machete. I hear a loud whoosh as both Max and Micah are transformed into their true height of fifteen feet, white wings a full twenty-two feet across from their furthest points. Both carry shields that are ten feet long and five feet across and fierce swords. Their eyes are focused on their opponents and the intersection becomes a type of coliseum. Interestingly enough, this war is only for the principalities to see the strength of the Christian and the might of the angelic forces. None of the humans can see this battle; however, they can feel the tension on the street.

Bennett continues, "They will fight to the death—usually that of their opponents. But they will become confused and quickly tire when they have multiple commands to obey simultaneously. This also happens when they are told to observe and draw conclusions. Thought wears them out quickly and that fatigue affects every part of their bodies. Do not be afraid. Let the battle rage for a few minutes and then give them three commands that are unrelated to each other. They will be on the ground in thirty seconds. Have Max and Micah take off their heads and throw them into the laps of those on the thrones. Make it messy. All will be distracted, and you can walk on."

The blows begin in earnest. Idiotis swings his 8-foot club at Max. For his great bulk, he is surprisingly graceful. Max backs up and feigns to the right. Moronicus waves his machete in the air, back and forth, attempting to intimidate Micah. Moronicus steps in and Micah moves forward, swinging his blade hard to meet the weapon of Moronicus. Idiotis is too close to Max for Max to use his blade and just as Idiotis swings his club, Max lifts himself off the ground thirty feet. Although the battle is heated and intense, Max can't help but laugh at how mismatched this fight is.

Then Idiotis looks at me with his one eye. He smirks. I have always been their intended target and Max's flight has left me unprotected.

I quickly shout instructions. They are advancing toward me to attack but they have to stop and listen. The instructions are simple, but they are complex in that there are multiple instructions requiring quick memorization and mental processing. Each command is given before the previous one has been completed.

I shout, "Moronicus, drop and give me thirty push-ups.

"Idioticus, give me thirty sit ups."

"Moronicus, I need a glass of water!"

"Idioticus, what is the square root of 37 times 6 minus 3 divided by 4?"

Thirty seconds later, the giants are staggering, holding their heads as if in great pain. Their weapons fall to the ground. They are moaning softly as if thinking takes all their strength. Max is by my side and I quietly tell him and Micah to decapitate their challengers.

"Toss them like bowling balls into the laps of Slavery and Murder." And it is done, blood and brains splash in all directions. A little of the spray has hit all of them.

The regional principalities and rulers of darkness are scrambling, but there is fury in their eyes as they wipe the mess off their clothes. Max and Micah whoosh down to their 6-foot height and are seen once again as normal tourists.

We turn our eyes to the man we are there to meet. He sees the three of us coming and extends a metal dish to us. He begs for a living and is hoping to obtain sustenance from the three tourists walking toward him. Instead of dropping a few shillings into his cup, I bend down to talk. His eyes widen in fear. No one talks to him. Ever. No one even looks at him. He is dust under their feet, long ago abandoned by family and forced to beg in a city where he is invisible.

My presence beside him in the street is not only alarming him, but many of the people on the street and those exiting the mosque are also taking notice. Some think I am an easy mark, while others are suspicious of us simply because we are strangers.

I ask him his name. He tells me it is Sayid, which in Arabic means "master". I can see that the man, Sayid, is anything but the master of his own circumstances. He says he begs here because of the foot traffic and because the authorities won't allow him around the city center where the streets are so narrow that only pedestrians can travel there.

I tell him that my name is Priscilla and that the Lord has sent me to Zanzibar to speak with him and, if Sayid is willing, to heal him. Can he imagine how it would feel to walk on two feet and normal, strong legs? Can he imagine working at a trade, or traveling to the market without having to rely on the kindness of strangers to provide for him? Can he imagine what it would be like to meet the eyes of another man at the same level? Can he imagine not turning away in shame from eyes that narrow and judge at the sight of him?

His eyes fill with tears and I can see that his fear is real. As easy as my questions should be to answer, they are not easy for him. He has never had a normal life. He has not seen life from the height of a "normal" man. He has never allowed himself to imagine what could never be. Slowly, however, Sayid begins to nod his head.

"I am here in the Name of Jesus Christ, who loves you and gave His life for you. He is the Son of God and He died to free you from every sin—thought, word, and deed that you could ever commit. Do you believe that?" I ask him.

Tears stream down his face as I reach over and take his filthy hand in mine. He murmurs the word "*ndiyo*", "yes", and there is hope in his eyes.

By now there are several people witnessing our discussion. Some are curious, others are skeptical. Some are fearful and some are angry at the mention of the name of Jesus.

I take his hand and I begin to pray in perfect Swahili. "Lord, I thank You for Sayid. I thank You that You knew him before there was an Earth for him to call home. I thank You that You love him with an everlasting love and that it is Your desire for Sayid to live with You in Heaven for all eternity. Heal him, Lord, from the crown of his head to the soles of the feet that You alone can create." As I begin to pray, Sayid's eyes widen as legs begin to grow inch by inch, until his thighs meet new knees, and knees become shins and calves, meeting new ankles, and ankles become feet with toes.

Sayid moans, panting with amazement. I continue, "Sayid, in the Name of Jesus, stand and walk."

He slowly stands to his feet. His eyes fill with joy and his face is bathed in light. Raising his arms in the air as he looks to me and then to Heaven. "Jesu, asante, asante, asante sana!" "Thank You, Jesus!"

The crowd now surrounds us but moves back in shocked amazement as Sayid begins to jog and dance. I look around, there is a woman hobbling toward us with braces on her lower legs. With a touch of my hand and the name of Jesus, she too, begins to dance as her braces drop to the ground, no longer needed.

I can hear the people asking each other what is happening. They begin to push their way to the front to see with their own eyes. One by one, people with varying types of diseases and infirmities, injuries and deformities, come up to be touched and to learn about the Son of God.

The scene on the street visibly affects the men coming from the mosque. The Spirit of the Lord has healed a few of them as they approach. Many others have family members afflicted by sickness, and are beginning to hope for them, even as they ponder a name that is not welcomed on the streets of Zanzibar—Jesus. A few others are in a rage. "How dare you minister to anyone, especially a filthy beggar outside of a holy place, our mosque, and during Ramadan, no less?" They begin to grab sticks.

A fifth principality joins the other four and his name is Islam. He is a brown-skinned man dressed completely in black from head to toe. On his head is a black turban. He wears a black tunic that flows down below his knees over black pants. His beard is graying, and his eyes are black. In his hand is the curved blade of a scimitar. He stands as he looks down, watching the war on his streets. He is the king reigning here and his is an iniquitous stronghold over the people of Zanzibar. His spirit has been radicalizing the people, calling for jihad and the destruction of all exceptions to jihad, including Christians, Jews, Hindus, and moderate Muslims.

The gradations of darkness in the sky begin to roll like a pot of water boiling on a stove. The sky looks as if it has a life of its own. Many of the angelic warriors are in the air, swords clashing. The enemies of the Lord are furious. Some are battling on the ground as the demons come up through the sewer drains. The fury of the spirit behind Islamic terrorism is battling with machetes, knives, and flamethrowers. Their hatred is palpable, thickening the air. I glance up to the thrones and see that all the principalities, powers, and rulers of darkness are on their feet. They gaze down in disbelief at the war waging below them in the street they consider to be theirs.

Everywhere I look, I see angels and demons in battle. I see people being attacked, even as their angels defend them. The angels have their shields up and see the strategy of the enemy before it is imagined. Demons lay dead and dying everywhere but still they continue to fight, their replacements seemingly inexhaustible. They are being observed by their rulers and to retreat would mean a death far worse than what the angels will extract from them.

Max and Micah call out to the warriors, giving directions to the angelic messengers on my behalf. The demonic horde have rightly guessed that it is my presence and the One who sent me that has caused the trouble for them today. Surrounded by warrior angels, nothing can penetrate the circle of protection around me. Gradually the battle begins to turn as the spiritual battle against the stronghold shifts. The people on the street are amazed at the goodness of God and their eyes are opened to the Way, the Truth, and the Life—Jesus. They turn to those who are angry brothers, neighbors, and friends. Slowly the eyes of most of them are opened.

The day is hot, but no one wants to go home. Still more people are rushing to the intersection, wanting to see with their own eyes what they have heard. We head to the churchyard into the church itself. More and more come to be healed. At the result of the healings, more and more want to hear about the Source of the healing—Jesus. I begin to preach. Soon people are falling to the ground unable to rise under the power of the Holy Spirit. People are being healed en masse.

As I look to the heavens, I see that all the previously reigning gods have left except Islam, who glares at me in rage. He lifts his scimitar in the air over his head and brings it down swiftly. I can feel the air movement even as he vanishes. It is a promise of retaliation. There is now a new throne over Zanzibar and a new King sitting upon it.

Through it all, Sayid is next to me, his eyes shining with joy and the in-person knowledge of the compassion of Jesus. We minister together, day and night, for three days. I turn to the church leaders and to Sayid and tell them that I will have to leave soon. I impart all that I received on the mountain, the day the 144 of us met with the angel and the Lord. As I turn to get some water and refreshment in the next room, I am amazed at the goodness of God and thankful to be used in such a way by Him.

I walk through the doorway into the church galley and instantly am translated back to my own little church. I am sitting in the same place and the same sentence being preached as when I prayed for the people of Zanzibar. The message is just beginning. I have not missed one word, even though I was gone three whole days in the spirit.

In the end, my time in Zanzibar resulted in 4,233 people healed of blindness, deafness, malaria, AIDS, tuberculosis, heart disease, cancer, orthopedic and neurological disorders, and injuries, and 12,501 accepting Jesus as Savior. The angels had been successful in their defeat of Slavery, Torture, Murder, and Antichrist in that region. The presence of the Lord replaced that of Islam. Once again, I thank the Lord.

"Lord, I offer myself a living sacrifice, pleasing to You. Please keep me pure in heart … "

The lady in the pew next to me looks at me at the end of the service and reaches out a hand to indicate there is a smudge of dirt on my cheek. She looks at me with questions in her eyes. Max and Micah smile from the back of the room, no longer seen by human eyes.

CHAPTER 7
KNOWLEDGE OF THE TRUTH

DAY 3, THURSDAY, AUGUST 13 - T MINUS 37
ANDEL LASKA
PRAGUE, CZECHOSLOVAKIA

I have heard it said that those living in the last generation are like the runners that are in finishing position, the anchor leg in a relay race. They are chosen for their speed and their agility. Not only do they have to be the fastest to cross over the finish line ahead of all other teams; they are also responsible for making up for lost time in the race and ensuring the baton crosses over without being dropped. Without the baton in hand, the race is lost, no matter who crosses over first.

There is work to do, and I am taking this forty-day mission very seriously. I am 47 years old and have lived in and around Prague, Czechoslovakia my entire life. During the first sixteen of them, I lived as a communist citizen, enduring rationing for controlled and limited resources, such as food, and suffering governmental control over nearly every aspect of life. In 1989, the Velvet Revolution brought an end to communism, and it is then that the nation split into two parts: The Czech Republic and Slovakia.

The end of communism brought changes to my way of life and those of everyone I knew. The government stopped being our provider and my father and mother were forced to work and worry about whether we would have enough to eat. They never knew if we would have money to pay for housing, heat, electrical power, and everything that we had had for "free" under the communist regime. It was an adjustment to lose what was wrong even when it seemed easy at the time. That was especially true when you've never known anything else. And it wasn't easy to have my school day cut short so I could go to work to help my parents feed our family because I was the oldest of four children.

It is ironic to me that after everything my people have endured that there are again changes in the air. The familiar feel of governmental control seems to be returning as a One World Government is argued and debated in the international courts. It is said that having centralized leadership will reduce the cost of government while ensuring fairness in the distribution of resources such as food and fuel. They promise security from terrorism. They promise financial security for each person in the form of an RFID chip inserted into the right hand or forehead, which will hold medical, financial, and demographic data, eliminating identity theft and the need for cash, credit cards or checkbooks. The Mark of the Beast.

For now, I will continue to focus on my mission, one day at a time.

I have done reasonably well in life. I work for an information technology company in the Czech Republic. I am married to my wife, Sophia, of eighteen years and we have two daughters ages fifteen and twelve. The end of communism and giving my life to the Lord have changed my life considerably.

One night when I was eighteen, I had a dream and Jesus himself sat at my bedside to talk with me. He said that when people rely on the government for everything they have, shelter, food, education and medical care, they begin to think of that government as their god. That god determines what a person believes, what they can say, what they can read, what they can think and what they can worship. He said that He was there at the very beginning with His Father and that together they created the earth and everything in it, including me. He told me about Adam and Eve and the point in time when sin entered the world. He described in detail the path for the world because of sin and how 2,000 years ago, He came to die a horrible death on a Roman cross. It didn't end there.

His Spirit battled with the Devil and his minions … and won. By the dynamite explosive power of the Holy Spirit, He came back to life again after three days in the grave. He traded His life for mine and set me free for eternity. His victory is my victory. He is more than worthy to be the only God that I worship forever, and no man or government has the right or authority to usurp it. I have been a believer ever since and will tell anyone who will listen to the Truth of Who He is.

The night on the mountain reinforced everything He said to me. He had told me that I had an awesome destiny and a role to play in His end time gathering of people chosen to be His from before the beginning of time. I was not surprised to be there, but I was in awe of Him and all I witnessed two nights ago.

My first assignment was last evening when I was pulled through a rainbow portal in the sky. I was rendered speechless to see it but to be sucked into it absolutely flabbergasted me. The colors inside it were unbelievable and some of them I have never seen on Earth. The sounds inside were the noises of battle and I hoped I would be ready when I arrived at my destination.

71

I landed in England in the last half of the sixteenth century to speak with a soon to be appointed advisor to King Edward who took the throne after his father, Henry VIII, had died. There was much to undo in the faith and in government. The Advisor was terrified at the discussion, but the truth resonated with him, deciding that even if he died a horrific death, he would be righteous in it. As a result of his courage and obedience, the church laws of England were overturned and literally thousands came to see Jesus as the King of kings and worthy of their praises. The victory was short lived, as was King Edward's life, but those gathered into the Kingdom were the assignment and it was achieved.

Now, I eagerly anticipate another evening speaking with kings. I get myself ready for bed knowing that when it is time to go through that portal again, I will be ready.

I go to sleep immediately, more fatigued than I thought when suddenly, at precisely 2:22 a.m., I am wide-awake. I get up for a glass of water, but as I open my bedroom door, I walk into a very well-lit room with white painted walls and mint green tiled floors. I am wearing a suit and tie and the guardian angels I met last night, Elsa, Jake and Rebekah are nearby, wearing lab coats.

As I look around the room, I can tell nothing from it. I don't know the year, the time, the type of place I have been brought to or whom I am here to help this evening, also known as "the target," as Mission Headquarters refers to them. There is another man in the room with me who looks dazed and a little fearful. It appears that he has been brought through a heavenly portal, a bridge from his world into the world of the assigned target, as I have.

Suddenly Bennett begins to speak to me. "The year is 2002 and you are visiting a mental health hospital in the State of New York."

He shows me the place where we are, a mental health institution, and a map of the inside. I can see a thermal image of a person pacing slowly, his heart beating furiously. Bennett tells me that this is my assignment for the evening and that he will be brought to me in the next few minutes. He then introduces me to the man across the room whose name is David. He is one of the 144 but tells me that all the work will be done by me this evening. David is here as an observer only, something that I admit, I think is strange. The words of the angel on the mountaintop were pretty clear in that we had all chosen to be used in the last times. Why would anyone need to observe only?

I look up to see a tall slightly overweight African American middle-aged man walk in. Bennett continues talking about the assignment. "His name is Rodney Freeman, and he was admitted twenty-five days ago with alcoholism and paranoid schizophrenia. He trusts no one and feels everyone is out to kill him, especially the nurses and other staff at the hospital. He was diagnosed with paranoia three years ago. You would never guess it to look at him now, but he worked for a major computer company until just under four years ago and was the top salesperson in the country for three years straight. He was married with a beautiful wife and has three children who are now fourteen, twelve and nine.

People, especially those who treat these kinds of disorders, always want to determine a trigger point. What happened to flip the switch? Were illicit drugs involved? Was it a traumatic event? Did his wife leave him? Did a friend betray him?" The man looks bloated with very little muscle tone. His expression is flat. His shoulders are slumped as if he is totally defeated.

Bennett continues, "He is being treated with antipsychotics, which is why the weight gain, flat affect and drowsy appearance. Every now and then, his eyes narrow and his face becomes angry. He sits up straight, fists clenched, and he looks like he will hit someone near him soon.

At that point, a staff member comes into the room and restrains him physically until he can get control over his actions. If this doesn't work, he is given an intramuscular injection and full leather restraints are applied. He will be taken back to his room."

Bennett looks over to David and Andel, "You both have a pair of glasses in the pocket of your jackets. Put them on and look at Rodney."

At that, I am able to quite clearly see a hateful gargoyle on Rodney's shoulder. He is whispering into Rodney's ear and occasionally gives him a slap across the face.

Bennett continues, "The jerking movement has been thought to be a side effect of the medication but is really a physical manifestation of the entity in the spiritual realm that is taking over the communication with Rodney. Rodney doesn't have a clue where the voices are coming from. He believes the doctors when they tell him in a lucid moment, that these are his tormenting thoughts that he can hear audibly—auditory hallucinations. The demon has told him that he is worthless, a victim of others, especially over those in authority over him; that he is right to not only defend himself but proactively attack. The spirit tells him that revenge is necessary for the evil behavior of others toward him to cease, and that he has the power to protect himself from those who intend to do him harm.

Rodney has lost his job, his wife, his children, his bank account, and the power over himself to improve his situation. He is in the hospital against his will, having been institutionally committed for psychiatric care by the authorities. Rodney is a believer. His successful life was a sign and wonder to those who didn't believe in Christ. His life was a testimony of the goodness of God. He had been a wild child, born on the Westside of Chicago, a witness to drug deals, prostitution of his own mother and sister for drugs, murder and rape. Boys, when he lived in that neighborhood, were expected to have a life expectancy of less than twenty years old.

His aunt took him one summer day to live with her in a small Indiana town. She taught him about the Lord, and he talked about how he wanted his life to be. He changed the way he thought about school, a career, women and his own body, graduated from high school and attended college. From the moment his mind was changed, his life followed. His path turned a full 180 degrees.

The enemy of his soul was furious, but patient, thinking that soon he would revert to the life he had known. It didn't happen. The Devil watched his job success, the courtship of his wife, the birth of his children, and then at the pinnacle of his life, he determined to destroy Rodney's life, taking his faith with everything else."

Bennett finishes with, "According to Romans 8, the enemy can't take his faith and that in itself, is victory!"

Then, quoting the Apostle Paul:

> "So now I live with the confidence that there is nothing in the universe with the power to separate us from God's love. I'm convinced that his love will triumph over death, life's troubles, fallen angels, or dark rulers in the heavens. There is nothing in our present or future circumstances that can weaken his love. There is no power above us or beneath us—no power that could ever be found in the universe that can distance us from God's passionate love, which is lavished upon us through our Lord Jesus, the Anointed One." [11]

"It is necessary for Rodney to be reminded who he is and Who is in him. That is your assignment tonight."

David looked at me and raised his eyebrows. I found myself lifting my eyes to Heaven and praying for David, discerning that David and Rodney are in the same sinking boat and that only Jesus can rescue them and get them out sane and alive.

I take a seat across from Rodney and look at him. "My name is Andel Laska and these are my colleagues, David, Elsa, Jacob and Rebekah. I have been sent by God on an assignment to talk with you and explain the truth of your illness and your losses over the past four years. This is going to sound funny, but first I am going to deal with the demon on your left shoulder. It will be easier to listen to me without the distractions."

Rodney's eyes turned to rage, and his fists come up instantly to hit my face and stop my words. The expression on Rodney's face mirrors the expression on the gargoyle's face. The angels Elsa and Jacob stand to their full eight and nine feet tall as they grab Rodney's hands simultaneously. His eyes are shocked, again mirroring the eyes of the gargoyle.

"You! Spirit of fear, anxiety, depression, oppression, and any other spirit attempting to elevate yourself above the Holy Spirit that lives in Rodney now, I tell you to shut up, in Jesus' name and get OUT! Go to the dry places now and never return!"

In a firm but gentle voice I continue, "Spirit of shalom peace and joy, I loose you now, in Jesus' name. I loose clarity of thought and impart spiritual eyes to see and ears to hear what God is saying to you now. You have the mind of Christ, Rodney.[12] God didn't give you a spirit of fear, but of power and of love and of a sound mind."[13]

Suddenly, against his will but in obedience to God, the gargoyle lifts off Rodney's shoulder and flies off. He has no choice. As he leaves, Rodney's eyes clear and his expression becomes peaceful but engaged, no longer flat, enraged, or drowsy.

He looks up to the faces of the angels and his eyes remain wide as he says, "I'm okay now. I won't hurt anyone." Elsa and Jacob let him go and shift back to their human height.

Rodney looks at me and is totally engaged in the conversation, "You said you were sent here by God?"

"Yes. He knows the destiny that He has for you. You were a sign and a wonder to others who observed your success and the joy in your life, especially knowing from where you came. You were born not only to succeed in business, but also to bring many into the Kingdom of God. You have the ideal trait of being able to be all things to all people. You can identify with those who have lived in an atmosphere of poverty, murder, prison, captivity to drugs and prostitution and those in the highest income brackets, successful in business and family.

You have the grace, mercy, kindness and compassion toward others not to judge them in their failures or in their successes. It is imperative that you know that you never have to doubt or fear again. The enemy used a demon to cause you to question everything in your life and in the process stripped you of everything. You are a believer, so you know that the same power that raised Christ Jesus from the dead lives in you. That power has been called Dunamis, like dynamite, or like a nuclear explosion, but that's just because we don't have another more accurate term for it. The Holy Spirit brought Jesus back to life again by His own power. The Holy Spirit doesn't just "live" in you, it is like boiling lava, living and moving in you. You have more power in the nail of your little toe than Satan and all his principalities and powers and spirits of wickedness in high places do working together as a whole against you. Take every thought captive. Ask yourself who generated every thought. If it is not of God, send it packing and live in the truth that Jesus died to give you. Start looking at yourself in the mirror and see Him looking back, as the greater One lives in you always.

Know this, your healing and deliverance today are just the first redemptions of many. You will recoup all your losses. Your family will be restored. You will again have business success. You will live for the Kingdom of God and will build faith for many who have been deceived by the enemy. And you will receive finances seven times what the enemy has stolen from you—an abundance for every good work."

I ask, "How do you feel?"

"I have never felt better, and I can't thank you enough. Thank you, Father God!" Rodney's face is filled with joy.

I looked over at David and his face has a myriad of expressions, one after the other: confusion, unbelief, suspicion, amazement, and hope. I whisper a prayer to God saying, "Help him, Yah, to know who You are."

We spend another three hours ministering to Rodney. He has supernatural understanding of the years the locusts had eaten and the destruction that Satan had heaped upon him. We pray for a seer anointing on him to see and discern for others in his path, in addition to discernment over his own body and soul. We pray for wisdom to surround him as a force field shield, much like the swords we were given on the night on the mountain. A force field shield that draws good and perfect things to him while repelling what isn't his to bear.

By the end of our time, Rodney is transformed from a victim of the demonic realm and medicine's solutions for behavioral disorders. He is alive, eyes clear, mood pleasant and peaceful, and even his body looks strong and fit. He is the beneficiary of a transformative miracle and the doctors and nurses are puzzled and amazed. They plan to keep him one more night for observation but to release him tomorrow if he continues as he is now.

I turn to walk out of the hospital room door and Bennett tells me that not only is Rodney restored in every way but, like Job, he has received more than he ever knew before this came upon him.

Bennett shares Rodney's future with both David and me and says, "Besides going back to work in the business marketplace, he is also an ordained minister of the Gospel and he is unafraid of speaking to anyone in his path. In eighteen years, he brought 5,006 people to the Lord!"

I look over to David and smile, "I'll see you around, I hope."

I find myself in my own kitchen getting a glass out of the cabinet. It is now 2:30 a.m. and I am amazed at what the Lord can do in eight minutes. I climb back into my bed next to my wife and smile.

CHAPTER 8
LIGHT OPS MISSION REPORT OF DEEDS—DAY 3

SAME DAY
ISABELLA KRIEGER
CHICAGO, IL

Time is a funny thing.

We humans tend to think of it as a twenty-four-hour period of time separated into daytime and night. But did you know there are actually thirty-eight time zones? If each time zone were one hour apart, there would be twenty-four in the world. The general rule is one hour for every fifteen degrees of longitude, but some time zones are only 30 or 45 minutes apart and in some very large countries, such as Russia and China, there is only one time zone for the whole nation. And there are three time zones along the International Date Line. My point here is that the length of my day during this forty-day assignment will not be twenty-four hours long but potentially much longer. This, however, is a time of redemption ... of both lives and time. While we are busy redeeming lives, God is redeeming time, and mine as the Recorder, too.

When He said a day was like as a 1,000 years and 1,000 years as a day, He meant it. When He stopped time to accommodate a battle victory or sped time up to win a foot race against a chariot, it gave precedent to stretch time for both the task and the recording of the results.

I am again in the Library of Heaven where my duties as Recorder of Deeds takes place. A fire continues to burn brightly in the stone fireplace, and I am comfortably ensconced in my padded chair at the mahogany library table. My concentration is on overdrive and I am fully engaged in the task at hand.

During each of the forty days, the angels will give me their tallies. As a day ends for one of the Special Forces, another begins for another of the Light Ops Team. Deployments and missions accomplished occur all day long and the angels are the ones counting the targets and the ripple effects of souls for those targets forward, over the course of time. The history books will already have been rewritten. The old things will have passed away and behold, all things will have become new.

The first couple of days are slow in recording the deeds of the Light Ops team as there is much to understand and to witness first-hand in the windows of time. Some of those windows cover almost two thousand years with many generations of change and positive consequences to observe. There are potentially millions affected, as each "ripple effect" has ripples of its own. Other assignments will be for a single target, perhaps on their deathbed. And once the goal is achieved, the assignment for that day for that Troop will be completed. That record update will take thirty seconds or less.

The Lord redeems the time in my work, as He is doing in each of the lives of the Special Forces. If done in consecutive seconds of time, every one of our assignments would take hours, days, weeks, and sometimes years. Even my role as Recorder of Deeds would take much longer if everything were done linearly and not in redeemed time. It is imperative to the Lord that we maintain our lives, jobs, and relationships; praying for grace for those people and things we see that require abundant grace in these last days.

Once I have recorded the deeds of the Light Ops Special Forces, the names of every person added to the Kingdom of God will be recorded in the Book of Life. The number of souls added to the Roster of the Kingdom will be so significant that the angels assigned as scribes will be recording the names until the end of the age.

It is extremely important to record each of the assignments, the goal of each mission, the accomplishment, and the impact to the citizenship rosters of Heaven. Even so, I want to pay attention to the events taking place. I want to take note of the ones that touch my heart and the ones that stimulate my soul, my mind and my emotions. I want to rejoice with the angels of Heaven and the Great Cloud of Witnesses as the purposes and plans of God are achieved. I want to laugh with glee as eternity changes for those who would have been lost were it not for the goodness of God in this mission to leave no one slated for Heaven behind, imprisoned forever in chains, fire and darkness.

The assignment that catches my attention today is undertaken and accomplished by a Special Forces member from Estonia, Liis; a girl of twelve. Her mission, after her transformation into a beautiful woman of thirty-three years old, is in Yemen. The year is 2011 and Liis is in the middle of the Yemeni Revolution, the Egyptian Revolution, and the Tunisian Revolution. All over the Middle East there are Muslim uprisings—the Arab Spring. Her assignment is one young man who will transform the hearts of many and in the Lord's time, will start a domino effect of hearts changed throughout the Middle East in nation after nation. He begins a cascade of one life working to change one life and pretty soon millions of people are radically changed.

It is a gift to me to be able to witness the before and after of millions of people, each walking their journey from darkness to light. I wipe away a tear of joy as I whisper a prayer of gratitude.

CHAPTER 9
THE SPIRIT OF THE AGE

DAY 4, FRIDAY, AUGUST 14 – T MINUS 36
DAVID ELI
NEW HAVEN, CT

As I tossed and turned, my night was filled with nightmares. There were three of them altogether, and they came one right after another. All different but with a common thread. I was the perpetrator of a sinister deception. I woke after each feeling unsettled, as if I had participated—no, planned and executed—in agreement with insidious evil in my own demise and that of many others.

My day was chaotic. I woke up that morning irritable and late for my first class. I am a professor of philosophy at one of the Ivy League Universities in its Divinity School and, until the night on the mountain, had spent my 30-year career using the Bible, the Koran, the Buddhist Tripitaka, the Hindu Vedas and Bhagavad Gita, the Zoroastrian Avesta and the sacred texts of many other religions, for and against themselves in an effort to disprove the hierarchy of God—any god—and man. I crafted a theological tug of war. Like a testimony used in court from unrelated sound bites, the words I used were taken out of context to form a totally different meaning. The purpose: to prove an untruth and disprove The Truth.

The night on the mountain blew me away. Seeing Jesus "in the flesh", along with the Great Cloud of Witnesses and hearing the words of the angel about the forty-day assignment caused a cognitive and spiritual dissonance in me. I am no longer comfortable in my own skin, much like a lesser version of Judas Iscariot before he hung himself to find relief from his own conscience.

It is extremely difficult for me to believe that I signed up for this before the world was even created. Was I wiser eons before I was born than I am now, eons later? What did I know then that I still don't know now? There are two extremes along the continuum of faith. One extreme is belief in Jesus, angels, creation and a timeline for His return. The other is the one I have lived most of my adult life, that there is nothing and no one but me as "god". I have been very comfortable in that place. If I could go back to the mountaintop and refuse the mission, back out, go AWOL, I would. As I observed the others, they looked as if they understood their purpose and had a lifetime of history to back up their duties. As it is, I have no foundation and spent last night—the first real assignment, with one of the Special Forces from the mountain to help give me a baseline.

I spent the first assignment day with a guy named Andel Laska and much of the time was spent arguing his idea of truth after our assignment of the night, a paranoid schizophrenic named Rodney. Jesus is the Son of God, who came to earth to save all people from their sins. Things like Creation, the Great Flood, Satan, and the existence of Heaven and Hell are all very real to him. I must admit that he and his assignment have caused me to at least consider that he might be right and that I have been wrong my entire life. Frankly, I am beginning to wonder if these forty days aren't to bring *me* into the Kingdom as another's assignment for redemption—the "Target".

It has been my life's purpose to "coexist"; to bring the world's religions into one in order to unify the world and in the process remove disunity and the violent passion created by it, homogenizing all. The wars over much of history have been caused by religion. If we can remove the differences, we remove the division and men can get along and celebrate the commonalities. Right?

In truth, my goal *is* coexistence, not to discover Truth and then engage in a Great Commission to spread it. It is to acknowledge the truth of all religions as truth. Coexistence is to have one key to one door that houses all religions and all gods. The fact is, if the one true faith was behind a door and I had a key ring of keys, each corresponding to a different religion, god, philosophy or creed, it would take a long time of trying each to open the door to the Truth. Andel and Rodney have made me wonder about the size of my key ring.

I am in a position of influence and interact through education with hundreds of students, some formally and others just by occupying the same space. It has been my mission to seed alternative truths into their minds. So many come to the Ivy Leagues to expand their consciousness and find their own version of truth, not realizing that men like me are seeding a new uniformity by disruption. I am raising them up for the good of mankind, and for the good of each of them as individuals as well.

The fact is, I have studied the sacred texts and have come to the conclusion that God has spoken to man through the Word of God, the Bible. I also believe that people will see what they desire to see if they go in with certain expectations. Similar to using statistics as a tool, situations and findings can be manipulated to reveal what the person expects or hopes to see, especially if the person goes in to prove what he already "knows".

What I have found is what I have always felt. Man is god and God is plural, made up of many men who agree. The Bible even says so. Anything, any action, can be justified. Man may be sinful, but a god, not so much. Being a god removes the need for accountability to anyone or anything, except to each person's own self. It entitles me to anything I want while making me assume some responsibility for leaving the world better just for having had me in it. I have always loved John Lennon's "*Imagine*". No Heaven, no Hell, no religion, no possessions, no country. Nothing to fight for or to fight about. Utopia.

My name is David Eli and I am a 56-year-old Philosophy professor and a secular Jew. My father was a professor and his before that. Our craft is knowledge and facts and while there are at least two sides to every story, we sometimes subtly spin our version of truth—the "Eli filter" we'd call it—and change lives in the process, hopefully for the better.

Our family stopped following the God of Abraham, Isaac and Jacob three generations ago, preferring atheism and the oblivion of nothingness after death. Philosophy is a maze where God is a dead end. It is foolishness to believe in what your eyes cannot see: the sovereign Creator, Savior of the universe and Lover of men's souls. My father and grandfather wouldn't approve but I have subtly converted to agnosticism, or even better, that each of us is a god in our own right.

Today I got into a verbal altercation with a young woman, a student required to take my class as a divinity student. Interestingly enough, she is also Jewish. I think she thought I was a spy in the ranks, and I can't help but think she may be right: an atheistic human god who teaches philosophy to religion and theology students at an Ivy League

University. For those who wonder about the words "atheistic" and "god" in the same sentence when referring to myself and my own beliefs, it only means that I won't share my glory with another either, as the God of Abraham, Isaac and Jacob said on several occasions.

All day long I have had the words "Did God really say?" in my mind and realize that though the serpent spoke them to Eve, they are coming out of my own mouth to young men and women who are honestly seeking to learn the truth. The young woman's name is Ruth, a rare name for a young woman in the 21st century. I can see her searching my eyes to find the door to my motivations and whether my anti-faith disease is acute and temporary or chronic and terminal. She is cautious because some diseases are contagious, and she definitely does not want to catch what I've got … "that even the elect might be deceived"[14].

Ruth knows herself and what she believes. And she knows why she believes it. She looks me straight in the eye and I can see that she hasn't fallen under the idea that she is lower on the totem pole because she is the student and I am the professor. There is no hierarchy here. No one is superior and no one is inferior. We are each one hundred percent accountable for the condition of our own mind, will and emotions. Or, in other words, we are accountable for our own souls.

Not everyone has the spiritual maturity that Ruth possesses. Her keen observation scrutinizes my soul and my motivations. With a single word, "Why?", she has made me feel ashamed of myself. Man sees the outside appearance, but God sees the thoughts and intents of the heart.[15] Ruth possesses the wisdom to see the heart.

The uneasy, disturbing feeling follows me the rest of the afternoon and by evening I want to be alone, safe in my apartment with a glass of wine and a good book. Once there however, no matter how many times I reread the same paragraph, I just can't concentrate on the words. I decide to go to bed to escape my unsettled thoughts, my anxiety and uncertainty growing, my conscience pricking me. In an especially weak moment, I even considered praying for both relief and protection, feeling almost as if I am in danger of some kind. Soon I am fitfully sleeping.

I enter the first of three disquieting dreams.

In this dream I am both the central character and the observer. The words of Genesis in the Garden of Eden in the temptation of Adam and Eve are the narration in the background of the dream.

> *"Now the serpent was more crafty than any beast of the field which the Lord God had made. And he said to the woman, "Indeed, has God said, 'You shall not eat from any tree of the garden'?" The woman said to the serpent, "From the fruit of the trees of the garden we may eat but from the fruit of the tree which is in the middle of the garden, God has said, 'You shall not eat from it or touch it, or you will die.'" The serpent said to the woman, "You surely will not die! For God knows that in the day you eat from it your eyes will be opened, and you will be like God, knowing good and evil."* [16]

In this dream I am the serpent, not only questioning but manipulating, deceiving and trying to cause disobedience and rebellion. In the process of destroying the potential of the couple I am meeting with in the Garden of Eden and their generations forever, I will also crush the hopes of God because He intensely loves these people that He has created. In time, as the serpent, I will bring the entire world to its bloody end.

Immediately after the first dream ends, I enter the second.

In this dream I am the figure in the seat of power. I am a king and a demigod. I have taught, manipulated, coerced, decreed and ordered the building of a great tower that will reach all the way to Heaven. Not in reverence, but in rebellion.

I am Nimrod.

In this dream, I again work to convince those that have a gold standard of belief. They either believe something with all their hearts, or they believe it half-heartedly. I convince them both to change what they believe, like an evangelist. Those who have no convictions are easy; they will go whichever way the wind blows. Plus, I am a king. Those who believe they have a choice are sadly mistaken. Finally, I am not fully human. I am half man and half fallen angel, on my father's side. Technically, we are not equal in our DNA, but it does give me power in this fallen world.

My goal is to kick God in the teeth, figuratively, of course. The words "I saw Satan fall like lightening", will be spoken in the future by The Son, but the fact is, it has already happened. I want to show God that, when we the people want to do something, and we agree on how and why, we can do anything. And it would have worked had the Godhead stayed in Heaven and not come down to see what we were doing. The confusion of the language made it impossible to execute our plan.

I wake again feeling very unsettled and afraid. I feel that I have been operating in disobedience and against myself in the process; as if I know it is wrong but am unable to turn back.

The third dream is short but terrifying.

I am dying and as my soul leaves my body it is taken swiftly and without mercy to the place of Judgment. I look into the fiery blue eyes of The King and I am very alone. No lawyer. No advocate. No one with whom to share the accusation and legal defense strategy. His voice is like thunder, stern and uncompromising. He tells me that I have been an influencer on earth by way of my students finishing the jobs their parents had begun, raising the youth on my university campus. I had the option of telling them the Truth but instead *chose* to perpetrate a lie. I had mocked them, reminding them that they were too old to believe in Santa Claus or the Easter Bunny. How could they believe in the virgin birth, miracles, raising people from the dead, the Great Flood, or the Triune God? I had intentionally deceived and worked day and night to persuade those of faith to desert it and I had committed the spiritual murder of innocents. I had affected the lives of hundreds of young people and my sentence would be very harsh as a result.

I awoke before I heard that I would spend eternity in Hell's lower levels. Not because I had murdered or raped, but because I influenced the innocent to cut themselves off from Him for eternity. I was drenched in sweat, heart racing with terror and the knowledge that there had been no misunderstanding. I was accused, judged and sentenced righteously.

Meeting Ruth today and knowing that she saw through me to the thoughts and intents of my heart, has me remembering and questioning everything. I recount every thought, word, and deed over much of my adult life. Last night on my first assignment with Andel Laska, I had been his Target. The discernment that Ruth has is the same that Andel had.

My shift from the faith in the God of my Fathers, Abraham, Isaac and Jacob, to believing in the possibility of anything or nothing was pretty large. But my philosophy has regressed to the belief that there is a god and I am a part of him. Which makes me a god in my own right. There is no authority higher than me, which means there are no standards other than my own that I need to live by.

The final shift is the malicious intent to perpetrate the lie through influence, persuasion and education of a generation of young victims. Education of students that doesn't include The Truth is definitely not a victimless crime. But the knowledge that I have been playing into the hand of pure evil to derail the destiny and eternity of a generation feels like spiritual genocide. These kids are also the future leaders of the world and godless leaders do no one any good, they are a betrayal to the land for which they are responsible. I know I am not alone in this assignment of evil, but it doesn't make me feel any better.

The only thing that brings me comfort is the knowledge that it is not too late to shift the other way. I had, like my father and grandfather, taken a purposely different perspective and made it a "kind" of truth. I could now choose to stand in my rightful place and see the past, present and future from God's perspective. This knowledge has caused a window to open into my own life to witness my own errors of thought and belief and then to see the actions I had taken based on those errors. I see my life pass before me in thought, word, and deed as if I am a speeding train. There has been so much evil manifest through my choices.

I think again of Judas Iscariot and feel the presence of an evil being in the room with me. He is mocking me. What right do I have to live? It is already too late. So many lives destroyed. Do I really believe God will forgive and pardon me? Why not take the path Judas took? Why not end it all and feel the true peace of nothingness? The Spirit of Death is near. He has condemned me and is urging me to condemn myself. I almost feel as if he is pushing me to end my own life because of the influence I hold and the availability of the youth I teach. If I were to change my ways and speak the Truth, I could undo much of the evil I have perpetrated. As hope fills me, the Spirit of Death leaves.

Suddenly, I find myself on the floor face down on the rug in my bedroom, weeping in repentance. Everything I'd seen through those windows that the Holy Spirit opened to my past life, I could repent for. Weeping harder, I finally feel some real Peace and I realize that sitting on the end of my bed is the God of Peace, Jesus Himself.

I look at Him in amazement and then hide my face. He knows me. He knows what I've done. He knows that I did it on purpose. And then I feel real fear. I feel His hand on the top of my head and He says the words He has used on hundreds of people while He walked the earth,

"Fear not. There is nothing done that cannot be undone. As important as your students are to Me, so are you to Me."

There is a part of me that wants to chatter, but all I can do is look at Him, eye-to-eye, Jew to Jew. I realize that this feeling of peace is not just a feeling and that He is actually talking to me without words. *Peace is a Person.* He is telling me He loves me and that no greater love has a man than One who gives His life for His friends.[17] He has given His for me and taken it back again to defeat death, Hell and the grave. He says that tomorrow I will meet the angels assigned to me and that the real work will begin but that my time will be redeemed. I will learn quickly, and revelation will be as quick as a thought.

I turn to look at the clock as He turns to leave. It seems as though He was only here for ten minutes, but four hours have flown by. As He leaves, He tells me that tonight I am the Target and as a result of tonight's successful mission, thousands will come into the Kingdom. The first one who will know it is Ruth.

I go back to bed for a couple of hours more of sleep and feel more peace than I have felt in decades. The Lord continues to talk with me in my dreams and my spirit hungers for more revelation.

I can't wait for tomorrow.

CHAPTER 10
LAODICEA DU MARE

"I don't know what I'm doing here but I want to know. *Why me?*"

My name is Thomas, which means "twin". I am not one of two but sometimes I feel like I am a man with two minds. Seven days ago, I was yanked out of bed on a sunny Saturday morning. I was slightly hung over and nearly sick in the bright, spinning portal that dumped me on the mountaintop with the others. It still freaks me out when I think about it. All my life I've had God forced down my throat— my parents are missionaries, for Heaven's sake. I lived in the wilds of Lesotho, Malawi and Mozambique until I turned fifteen. Then we moved to Amsterdam where my parents were born. Cool place unless you're a geeky kid without a wardrobe, a language or a history with the people you suddenly find yourself surrounded by. The transition from one world to the next took my parents about fifteen minutes, but I am

29 years old and still *think* in the Zulu language. I never knew anything else. My transition has taken nearly fifteen years and still I find myself uncomfortable in crowded restaurants, busy traffic and grocery stores. I could blame my parents for their lack of sensitivity regarding their only son, but I blame the One behind them … God.

The portal, the mountaintop, and the forty days of assignments are pretty interesting, I must admit. And I can feel the spiritual urgency, whether I want to or not. The fact that I was chosen for God's Special Forces, however, must be a joke. If God can hear my thoughts, He knows how far I have gone to get away from Him. I have questioned whether He even exists and how a God who is Spirit can have a Son in the form of a Man. He has seen the lengths I have gone to so that I can live my own life completely away from the life my mother and dad chose to live and the knowledge I had of Him in my early life. I think He has chosen badly in choosing me, if in fact He did "before the foundation of the world". But the thought that I would volunteer for this is *very* hard to believe. Why would I volunteer to live my last days as a missionary after spending the last fifteen years trying to unlearn what I lived for the first half of my life as the only child of missionary parents?

Still, it is difficult to unlearn what you learned early on as The Truth. I have found myself over the last few months when I am completely alone and my thoughts are all mine, talking to God as if He was really there, almost in my subconscious mind that peeks into my conscious thoughts. It is then that I feel anger at myself for being deceived and at Him for being the One Who deceived my parents and then me. If you're angry at Someone, that Someone has to exist though, right? The twins in my mind often struggle with thoughts and arguments of His existence. And no matter what, I always win … and I always lose.

Even so, the morning on the mountaintop was pretty cool. People who were just like me surrounded me that night. Only *they* had really wanted to be there. I was an imposter. I was probably the only one there that had gotten smashed the night before and woke with the need for a greasy cheeseburger to settle my hung-over belly, only to find myself in a portal of colored light, hearing amazing sounds of clashing swords as I swirled through time and space.

He was there. And I mean Jesus really was *there*. I still fight the truth in my angry moments, but I can't really deny it anymore. He is real and His love for me and for the people of the world hit me like a ton of bricks. The air was thick with that love. Even the memory brings tears to my eyes. In the middle of a sentence, He looked at me.

"You are no mistake for this assignment. I knew exactly what I was doing when I chose you."

This is day seven of forty and I feel ill equipped to handle these trips in the night. I have three angels with me at all times and I know I would already be dead without them. They are Michelb, Malachi and Elijah and they have fought unbelievable battles for me as I learn to handle the weapons for each journey. I heard the Lord talk to me quite clearly this morning. He knows everything so I know He can see my uncertainty with every part of this. He said,

"I know all. I see all. Nothing happens that I don't allow or know about in advance. When I speak to you, it strongly behooves you to listen and do, for I will not lead you astray. Your time will not be wasted. When I say that I have purposes, plans, callings and destiny for you, I mean it. I strew light into the path of the righteous.[18] I make the crooked places straight.[19] I am your rear guard.[20] I neither slumber nor sleep.[21] I Am your Provider, Strong Tower and Fortress.[22] When I tell you to do something, please do it. You are linked with many and will be linked to many more. Divine encounters and divine appointments are in your future to promote you and open many hearts to Me in the process. It is the hearts that I AM after."

I know some of the 144 can see things that can't be seen with the naked eye, but I think many of them have been practicing that form of seeing for many years. I have been "out of the life" for a long time and didn't have that gift even when I was living in it. I've been talking a lot with Bennett and he has given me what looks like a two-sided refractor—one of the tools an ophthalmologist uses when he flips one side up and the other down and asks which one you can see out of better. Only this one is like an eyeglass that shows you the supernatural world.

Yesterday I was walking near my target and Bennett told me to flip up the glass. The instant I did, I saw snakes everywhere under my feet and low flying vultures in the air, trying to keep me away from the guy I was there to see. When I flipped the glass down again, I saw grass, dirt and rocks. The glass was flipped again so that I could see what I needed to war against to get where I was going. Strangely enough, I was not afraid at all even though I *hate* snakes. My sword shortened to the length of a machete and I took care of them and the angels fought off the demonic birds.

I am standing near a coffee shop on one of Amsterdam's 160 canals, Prinsengraht, sipping a cappuccino. My bike is leaning against the bridge, and I am thinking about the amazing day I will have today. I am beginning to look forward to these forays into other parts of the world and traveling through time when I realize I've left my wallet in the coffee shop. I turn back and walk the 25 feet back to the doorway, and as I enter, I see the ground shift. There is no longer a coffee shop, no longer a canal behind me, and no need for a wallet. I walk out through a different doorway altogether.

I am now feeling the late afternoon sun warm on my face, facing the Mediterranean Sea in modern day Latakia, Syria, the ancient city of Laodicea du Mare. It is the fifth largest city in Syria after Aleppo, Damascus, Homs and Hama and it is in a state of chaos. I turn to face the city and see images of burned out buildings. The windows are like eyes; gaping, black holes of emptiness and death. Other parts of the city have fared better but even in neighborhoods where buildings are intact with palm trees neatly lining the streets, there is evidence of civil war and the knowledge that deep darkness is covering the people. Sirens fill the air, the occasional explosion heard and then more sirens. The streets are filled with traffic and horns honking but there are also the charred remains of cars that carried suicide bombers in several spots throughout the city. There has been a civil war going on for several years, the Syrian people against their corrupt and cruel government. A darker evil is here, as well, initially taking advantage of the unrest throughout the nation and trying to bring Jihad to all but the most fanatical Islamists, but now in full control.

The Islamist State—ISIS—along with four new Islamic organizations with the same mission statement, is committing genocide against all who oppose their theology including Christians, moderate Muslims and Yazidis. Their sentences include starvation, mutilation, torture, rape, crucifixion, and beheadings. Their tools of war include biological, chemical, nuclear and automatic weapons, knives, and swords. The media is used successfully for recruitment activities all over the world and as a tool to spread fear. This is an evil that seduces would-be anarchists, terrorists and murderers. Their enthusiasm is apparent in the videos they film of their own atrocities. ISIS was temporarily deactivated but has come back with a vengeance. They have taken control of Syria and have entered into Israel, Jordan, Iraq, and Turkey. There is no longer a government of Syria. It has bombed airports, train stations, stadiums and arenas. It has threatened the entire world and has acted on those threats in several European and American cities. Yes, *deep* darkness covers the peoples.

"Why am I here, Jesus? I did not sign up for this and I have no weapons to use to defend myself."

I hear His voice say, *"You are the light, Thomas. You volunteered eons ago and, frankly, you are one of My best. You are a warrior's warrior and I am so glad you are here. Did I not say that I would help? Did I not say that your success is guaranteed? Did I not say that not one hair on your head would be harmed? What I say, I mean. I honor My word over My name*[23] *... and My name is everything."*

Bennett tells me, "This is a coordinated effort tonight. There will be twelve of the 144 of you on this same assignment, though you will be positioned throughout the nation of Syria. Soon you will be meeting in the War Room of Heaven to get your orders. Once you are back with feet on the ground, you will not see each other until your assignments are successfully completed.

It is time for the leaders in strategic cities and regions—demonic strongholds of Syria to become followers of the One who came to save them more than 2,000 years ago. Tonight, they will all be like Saul on the road to Damascus, struck blind and isolated for their murderous ways, killing the people who worship our King. Instead of being tortured and then executed, they will be ministered to by angels and by you, Thomas."

The streets are ominously quiet, like a forest before an earthquake. The residents of this city feel the evil and hide behind their doors and covered windows. The Jihadists have only a short way to go to completely reign in Latakia. The entire nation of Syria is a Jihadist's stronghold in the world. Terrorism is a global issue, as everyone knows. The command center may be in Syria, but the targets are in Europe, Israel, Australia, Central and South America, and the United States of America, as has been seen time and again with all the Jihadi organizations, as started by

ISIS in the last two years.

I flip the glass up to see what I can't see with the naked eye and am horrified. The sky is swirling with black clouds that are knotted up into a carpet for a huge throne, surrounded on either side by two slightly smaller thrones. All three are occupied.

On the throne to the left of center is Islam, dressed totally in black, from the turban on his head to the shoes on his feet. His face is covered in a black wrap so that only his black eyes show. His hatred is palpable as he stares down at me. Elijah and Malachi have been watching him and are standing twelve feet tall as they walk on either side of me. Michelb walks ahead of us with his sword drawn. His posture and stance reveal his fearlessness to the ones on the thrones and to me.

To the left of the throne is a woman who is totally covered in black from the top of her head to her small feet and she is sitting uncomfortably, like a dog, at his feet. He has a rope around her neck and her hands and feet are bound in chains. Standing behind Islam are Slavery, Rape, Deception and Murder.

On the throne to the right of center is Vengeance. He is responsible throughout the world for immediate crimes of passion and for crimes of revenge that take years to execute. He is patient. He is rash and impulsive. His cells are woven from hatred and wrath and his face wears a perpetual snarl. He is covered by black leather slacks and a crimson coat—the color of all the blood he is responsible for shedding, since Cain murdered Able.

Standing to the right of his throne are Torture and Hatred. Seeing these emotions as the spirits they are, temporarily manifested in the flesh, is sobering. These guys aren't just "feelings". They are separate entities apart from flesh and blood man. They have been responsible for the atrocities throughout the world since man was removed from the Garden of

Eden. Its only when man agrees with the words whispered into their ears from these "things" that they become conjoined, wreaking havoc in the world. Prisons are full because man has partnered with Hatred, Wrath, Vengeance, Rape, Deception and Murder.

In the middle, sitting on the huge throne is Satan, himself. To say he is ugly is an understatement, though Bennett has told me that he can shape shift into the most beautiful of men, as he was when he was the light-bearer in Heaven, an archangel covered with jewels. His form was constructed from the musical instruments he used as the worship leader of God, the Father. Now he is wrinkled, and his face has a greenish tint. The color of chronic liver failure. His hands are like claws with long nails and on his head, he has two horns, like ram's horns that curl downward. He is ancient and his evil "anointing" is like an electrical pulse that can be felt and feared from miles away.

Bennett continues, "Often he delegates to his henchmen but sometimes he wants to be in the middle of everything. Tonight, in Damascus, Syria, there is a meeting of demonic forces who will strategize for the future of the world and Satan intends to rise up to receive accolades from his principalities and powers to declare and decree his plans for the destruction of the entire world. Fear, extortion and murder will ramp up to a new high, as these are the tools that have always worked best for him. He believes his plan will be fully in place, ready for the first step to be executed in 34 days. But as of tonight, many of his plans will be thwarted."

I feel the sound waves of Satan's presence. He looks down at me with jeering, much like Goliath looked at the shepherd boy, David. I feel the spirit of fearlessness surge through me and take over as I continue to walk up the streets of Latakia, Syria. We have been deployed here from Heaven and we walk in the authority of the One who sent us. Our mission is guaranteed but I am not complacent in that knowledge. My ears are open. My eyes are open, and my eyepiece is in place.

As we 'round a corner onto a road with burned out buildings, we can hear the gunfire increasing and explosions nearby. We enter a building through an open doorway to avoid exposure and suddenly all four of us are transported to the War Room of Heaven talking with Bennett "in the flesh".

Bennett stands about eight feet tall and he is dressed in combat fatigues, his hair is messy and wind-blown, and round eyeglasses framing serious and intelligent blue eyes. He is surrounded by technology, but these are computers and equipment I have never even imagined. He has angels sitting at terminals all around the room and a control console that views a huge map of the Earth.

In front of the map, rotating above a large pedestal is a very large hologram of a transparent Earth "globe" spinning on its axis, surrounded by its solar system. A dial sits nearby on a notepad in thin air that allows a timeframe to be chosen to reflect historical events or those in real and even future time. Situations are depicted with diagrams and colors, within and without the hologram, including natural disasters: meteors, volcanoes, earthquakes, tsunamis, tornadoes, hurricanes, blizzards, avalanches, and floods, throughout history. Other holograms are present showing catastrophic pestilence, wars, times of peace on the Earth, and man-designed and controlled disasters. Finally, they depict times and territories on the Earth when men believed in their King Jesus versus the darkest of times when men refused to believe.

These holograms could be situated one on top of the others to reflect geographical areas that were the darkest and most catastrophic. They also reveal those that were in peace because they were standing in the Light, much like the transparent overlays mapping the human body in old anatomy and physiology textbooks. Instead of overlays by bodily system, circulatory, nervous, integumentary, and so on, these holograms represent spiritual climates and consequences, positive or negative over time. The hologram that we are currently viewing is set to present day and the darkness over the earth is readily apparent in its appearance. There are natural disasters, plagues, extreme weather patterns, and wars over much of the globe as the world nears its end.

There are very small sections of light sprinkled over the surface of the globe. They represent the Body of Christ and the Light they carry within them. The Light Ops mission of the 144 Special Forces is to change the balance of darkness to light by rescuing the chosen so that they can join with the hosts of Heaven to ensure the destiny of those who will be the Lord's.

Also present in the War Room are 25 angels, each standing ten to twelve feet high in full battle array with what looks like Kevlar body armor and night vision glasses around their necks. The eleven men and women they protect are similarly dressed. I remember both the humans and angels from the mountaintop.

There is a large map of Syria and the surrounding nations of Turkey, Iraq, Israel, Lebanon, and Jordan on the wall. The map is covered with twelve circles or ellipses covering the full 71,498 square miles of Syria and into the nations surrounding it. The population within each circle determines the size of the circle. Larger circles have a lower population per square mile and smaller circles have a higher population. Less densely populated areas had shifted higher over the past few years due to refugee camps strategically placed outside of large population centers. Each circle overlaps slightly those around it. Each of us were to be assigned a circle and within that circle, the Jihadi leadership in control of that geographical territory.

My region is the northeastern Syrian Al Ladhiqiyah and Tartus provinces and into the Idlib and Hamah provinces, including the Mediterranean coast to the east, the northern Syrian-Turkish border, the southern Syria-Lebanese border and to the west about 50 miles from Homs and Hama.

Bennett begins to talk of the history in this region of the Earth and the impact of each layer of conquest and surrender from each historical point forward to present day. Like ripples in a still pond after a small pebble is dropped, the surface of the water will never be still again. As undulations in the surface of a lake caused by raindrops, so are the effects of each layer of history on this geographical pond. The history of this region—all regions of the earth—are affected by the course of events since the beginning of time. Some areas grow darker and others lighter based on their relationship with the Creator of the Universe. The human history of this part of the world, initially referred to as a region within Mesopotamia, is long, spanning six millennia.

Bennett gives the highlights of this part of the world's history in under fifteen minutes, but it becomes clear who the demonic regional principalities and powers are as time has progressed, "There have been people in the region since 4,000 BC. The Amorites lived here in 2,100 BC and then the Hittites from 1,500-1,300 B.C. The people suffered at the hands of the Assyrians, the Babylonians and the Egyptians while life improved somewhat under the Persian Empire. The Seleucidae, AKA the kings of Syria, followed a brief conquest by Alexander the Great. Then the Armenians, the Parthians and the Romans invaded the land.

Christianity began after Jesus' life, death and resurrection in the region. St. Paul was converted on the road to Damascus, but religion has been an important factor in the social and political fiber of this part of the world since the beginning of time.

The Amorites worshipped a pantheon of gods, as did the Hittites.

Their chief deity was Amurro, also known as Belu Sadi, the lord of the mountains, and his wife, Belit—Seri, the lady of the desert. They came from the land of Mount Hermon on Israel's far northern border with Syria, where the fallen angels fell to earth and mated with the sons of man, mentioned in Genesis 6. One of their kings, Og, was 13.5 feet tall and was a descendent of that unholy alliance.

There has been a United Nations presence at Mount Hermon for decades. Though there has been unrest in the region for hundreds of years, they also have a secret mission—they are here to watch for Apollyon, also known as Abaddon, the angel of the abyss, and his fallen angels, bound in the center of Earth since the days of Genesis. He is known in the Book of Revelation as the Destroyer and the UN are keeping their collective eyes out. Caesarea, at the foothills of Hermon, was once a worship center of every false god imaginable. The god Pan demanded human sacrifice in what was known then as the 'Gates of Hell'. Worshipping these regional false gods has set the tone for its chaotic and violent past, present and future. Thousands of gods representing weather, animals, sun, moon and stars, mountains, water, monsters, dragons, forest, destiny, wisdom and fertility were worshipped throughout the land. Named gods including Dagon, Nebo, Ashtaroth, Baal, and Bel are just a handful. In this region, the moon god, Sin, was also worshipped.

Bennett continued with the political and governmental history of the nation of Syria and the surrounding territories. "In the 4th Century after the division of Rome into Eastern and Western empires, Syria fell under Byzantine rule. In the 7th Century the Muslim Arabs conquered Syria and in the one that followed, most Syrians converted to Islam. There have been several cycles of division in the Muslim world as regional Islamic dominance shifted multiple times. The Crusaders invaded in the 11th—14th Centuries and fought the Seljuk Turks and in the 12th Century warred against Saladin, who was victorious over both Muslims and Christians. Because of pervasive disunity, Muslim against Muslim, the region was overrun in the 13th Century by the Mongols and later defeated by the Baybars, the Mamluk ruler of Egypt.

France, Turkey and Egypt each claimed them several times until 1944 when they were proclaimed an independent nation, but still internal national disunity reigned. The nation of Syria maintained its attitude of division, which caused it to abolish its parliamentary form of government for a dictatorship. They have had several unholy alliances with the nations of Libya, Egypt, Iran and the USSR, supporting terrorism. Syria has fought Israel in four wars over geographical territories. They continue to attack themselves from within and have even used chemical weapons against their own citizens. Their national instability has groomed the rise of terrorist organizations such as Hezbollah, Al Qaida, and ISIS within its borders.

Cycles of the worship of false gods, including worshipping their kings and presidents, mixed with national confusion and division against itself, along with the principality of radical Islam, has fostered chaos, war and slavery. The national and religious laws regarding women and one of their weapons of war, rape, is keeping this nation in darkness and their people in chains. The antidote to all of this is Jesus, the God of Peace, the Truth and the Light. Time is short now and the Lord needs His forces accelerated and multiplied in this hour."

The goal of our assignment is to turn the leadership from the dark, violent, deceived and demonic forces currently in command of the region, to the Light of Jesus Christ. These leaders are to be commissioned to lead those under their authority and those they previously persecuted, to the Way, the Truth and the Life. Filled with the Holy Spirit, they will treat all they will encounter with the love of Jesus of Nazareth, a Jew and the Savior of all mankind. Prior to our arrival, the ability of people of faith to visit the region and minister to the lost and the hurting, both victim and perpetrator was extremely difficult. Angelic visitors would minister to some and the Lord would appear to others in dreams and visions.

The fragrance of spicy balsam and frankincense wafts in as Jesus walks purposely into the War Room at that moment, also dressed in military fatigues. Each of us bows our head in awe and we feel His tangible love even as He begins addressing us as General of the Angel Armies.

Jesus asked the group, *"Do you remember the history of how Saul became the Apostle Paul? Saul held the coats of the men who stoned Stephen to death because of his faith in Me. He was in agreement with the men and was heartily glad they did it. This is recorded in the Book of Acts 7, 8 and 9. In Chapter 9, I grab Paul's attention and that is your assignment for the men you will be meeting this night."*

Suddenly the scripture fills my mind and I begin to recite from memory:

> *During those days, Saul, full of angry threats and rage, wanted to murder the disciples of the Lord Jesus. So, he went to ask the high priest and requested a letter of authorization he could take to the Jewish leaders in Damascus, requesting their cooperation in finding and arresting any who were followers of the Way. Saul wanted to capture all the believers he found, both men and women, and drag them as prisoners back to Jerusalem. So, he obtained the authorization and left for Damascus. Just outside the city, a brilliant light flashing from Heaven suddenly exploded all around him. Falling to the ground, he heard a booming voice say to him, "Saul, Saul, why are you persecuting me?"*
>
> *The men accompanying Saul were stunned and speechless, for they heard a heavenly voice but could see no one.*
>
> *Saul replied, "Who are you, Lord?"*

"I am Jesus, the Victorious, the one you are persecuting. Now, get up and go into the city, where you will be told what you are to do."

Saul stood to his feet, and even though his eyes were open he could see nothing—he was blind. So, the men had to take him by the hand and lead him into Damascus. For three days he didn't eat or drink and couldn't see a thing.

Living in Damascus was a believer named Ananias. The Lord spoke to him in a vision, calling his name. "Ananias."

"Yes, Lord," Ananias answered.

The Lord said, "Go at once to the street called Abundance and look for a man from Tarsus named Saul. You will find him at Judah's house. While he was praying, he saw in a supernatural vision a man named Ananias coming to lay hands upon him to restore his sight."

"But Lord," Ananias replied, "many have told me about his terrible persecution of those in Jerusalem who are devoted to you. In fact, the high priest has authorized him to seize and imprison all those in Damascus who call on your name."

The Lord Yahweh answered him, "Arise and go! I have chosen this man to be my special messenger. He will be brought before kings, before many nations, and before the Jewish people to give them the revelation of who I am. And I will show him how much he is destined to suffer because of his passion for me."

Ananias left and found the house where Saul was staying. He went inside and laid hands on him, saying, "Saul, my brother, the Lord Jesus, who appeared to you on the road, has sent me to pray for you so that you might see again and be filled to overflowing with the Holy Spirit."

All at once, the crusty substance that was over Saul's eyes disappeared and he could see perfectly. Immediately, he got up and was baptized. After eating a meal, his strength returned.

Within the hour he was in the synagogues, preaching about Jesus and proclaiming, "Jesus is the Son of God!" Those who heard him were astonished, saying among themselves, "Isn't this the Saul who furiously persecuted those in Jerusalem who called on the name of Jesus? Didn't he come here with permission from the high priest to drag them off and take them as prisoners?"

Saul's power increased greatly as he became more and more proficient in proving that Jesus was the anointed Messiah." [24]

Jesus continued,

"Your assignment will be to love these men as brothers and friends into My Kingdom and they will be responsible to turn others in these geographical areas. Not all will turn for many are fully deceived and totally persuaded that fanatical Islam is the way to Paradise. They are tares sown by the Devil in the earth now. Many, however, have been questioning and some are walking in pretense, knowing the Truth but seeking to preserve themselves in a position of influence to tell that Truth to both victim and persecutor. This night many of the influencers of the Jihadists in the land of its stronghold, the caliphate, will be turned to Me.

This day was strategically chosen for this assignment. There is a large meeting of the caliphate planned for tonight in Damascus. They gather to report the current status in each region and to determine a strategy for the invasion and destruction of the world, as it is currently known. That meeting will not occur however, as none of the local regional leadership responsible for executing the strategy will be available for it. In preparation for the meeting, each of the twelve Syrian local regions will be holding meetings of their own to discuss how to exaggerate their own successes and minimize their failures. Each of these meeting rooms will suddenly be filled with blinding light as I ask them why they continue to persecute Me and those I love. You will appear at these meetings immediately after their eyes are blinded. Chaos, confusion, and terror will ensue as the 25-50 men present in each meeting room attempt to escape without the benefit of sight.

The regional principalities, powers and demonic forces will be kept at bay and outside of the meeting halls. Angels will be deployed, wing-to-wing, around the exterior perimeter of the buildings. Others will be deployed to sweep the interior of the buildings for demons and destroy them on sight. Still others, directed by you, will escort each prisoner to an isolation room of their own.

This will be a divide and conquer strategy designed to determine the heart of each of these men. Some genuinely desire to be righteous but are following the wrong god and executing the wrong tactics. Others know full well that they are perpetrating evil and find joy in doing it. The evil ones will be collected in a prison for the remaining days of the Light Ops deployment. After the Feast of Trumpets, they will be released to terrorize again, and that terror will be ramped up with none in the Body to fast and pray for the deliverance of those left behind.

Those whose hearts desire righteousness, will be ministered to by both the human and angelic resources deployed for this assignment. They will have their physical needs met for food, shelter and sleep. They will have their spiritual needs met by intensive instruction about Me. The time will be redeemed with supernatural revelation. They will be loved into My Kingdom, a Kingdom without end. They will fight for peace and not for war. They will be trained in kindness and not torture. They will be instructed in grace and not judgment. And they will be deployed as leaders—shepherds—to gently lead the remaining lambs to Me. Their assignment will be very short, but it will be intense with many victories of souls to celebrate."

Suddenly, I am returned to the burned out building I entered only a short time ago. Michelb, Malachi and Elijah are with me. In the short time I have been gone, the streets of Syria have become the epicenter of evil. There is darkness everywhere.

The buildings on this street all look the same, their top floors imploded down into the levels below them. Roofs have caved in and crumbled from missiles shot from miles away, their windows like soulless eyes. The exposed rebar looks like scant eyelashes. The doors imploded and the overhangs dropped to the street below. The street has piles of rubble, cement, rock, and parts of buildings pushed off to the side so that cars and armored vehicles can move. There are burned out vehicles at the end of this street to act as a barricade to more destruction from cars used as weapons in suicide bombings.

Tall demons—eight to ten feet tall—surround Michelb, Malachi, Elijah and me and they lead us roughly into another building across the street, pushing and attempting to cause pain and fear. They apparently do not recognize my team as angelic forces. Believing instead that *they* are the ones who are stronger, larger and part of an organization that cannot lose.

This building is slightly more intact than the others. It is dirty and foul smelling and its atmosphere has more to do with the inhabitants of it than anything external. It smells like a mix of dirty, unwashed humans and the Spirit of Death, like roadkill on a 90-degree day. As we are led in as not yet interrogated prisoners of war, I see a large boardroom table with fifteen swarthy men seated around it. They are mostly dressed in khaki camouflage with black berets, but three are dressed in long black tunics over black pants with black turban-like hats and long beards. Half are smoking unfiltered cigarettes, which adds to the smell in the room. There are fifteen pairs of eyes on us and most are filled with rage. A few of them register our presence and their eyes are afraid.

I suddenly hear Bennett speak into my earpiece, "On the count of three, close your eyes tightly and keep them closed until I say to open them."

I smile slightly at those with fear registering in their faces. The smile is like gasoline on a fire to those with rage in their eyes. They rise to their feet issuing threats that would wipe the smile off the face of most people, especially without this godly assignment to keep them protected.

Suddenly, two spirits push me up against the wall. The first is Doubt and the second is Scorn. Doubt looks at me and asks on whose authority I have come. I am, after all, one who considers himself betrayed by God, forced to endure his parent's missionary life and then move to the western world, unsophisticated and unprepared. "Do you think God forgets that? If YOU were God, what would you do with someone like you?"

Scorn follows up with, "How can you expect this same God who sent you here to protect you? Don't you realize where you are and the power that is against you? Don't you know the consequences of turning your back and denouncing Him? You're going to die tonight, and your God is going to let it happen as punishment!"

Michelb, Malachi and Elijah rise to their full fifteen feet, wings fully extended around me. Doubt and Scorn move away from me as expressions of fear and astonishment pass over the face of each of these men.

All at once, I hear Bennett's calm voice say, "3 – 2 – 1. Now close your eyes tight!"

My eyes are clamped shut as tight as I'm able. I hear the sounds of fear as one by one they scream to shut the lights off. It is burning their eyes like acid and blinding them. Within ten seconds, the fear is more pronounced. Chairs crash to the floor as each try to rise out of their seats to get out of the room, but they are clamoring over each other, like the blind leading the blind, realizing that none of them can see anything at all.

Bennett says to open my eyes and see the chaos that is ensuing.

All of a sudden, Jesus walks into the room. The demons shriek in terror and run from the building. The Devil, observing from a corner of the room, looks with anger, his face snarling but with a hint of fear at the One who has completely changed the agenda for the night. The room is silent except for the panting of the men, whose chests are heaving in fear.

Jesus asks each man, calling them by name, "*Mohammed, Khalid, Tayyib, Adnan, Fathi, Sami, Ammar, Halil, Tarek, Akram, Nizar, Firas, Marwan, Ghaith, Majd, Alaa, Ahmed, Maan, Rifat, Houmam, Bassel, Sayid, Majd, Tayeb, Fatih, Abdel, Ghiyath, Jamal, Jibril, Misbah, Ibrahim, Habib, and Isam, Why are you persecuting me?*"

"Who are you?" they ask.

The responses are all the same, but the inflections are on both ends of the spectrum, one end afraid, meek and submissive and the other raging, accusing and threatening. It is at this point that the room is flooded with the angelic host, each dressed in Kevlar, ready for battle.

"All of you have choices", I say. "You can choose to follow the One who gave His life for you, or you can choose to follow the one who has hated you since you were a gleam in your father's eye. Tonight, the spiritual blinders come off and you will see the Truth. Some of you will shake your fist at Him in spite of what will be revealed to you tonight. I don't wrestle against flesh and blood but against principalities and powers and rulers of darkness in high places. There are consequences for choosing evil over Good. Jesus himself will make His decision regarding you. He sees even what you don't want Him to see and what you try to hide, but … "

The words are not mine, but I feel I know them well:

> "*With Him are wisdom and might; To Him belong counsel and understanding. Behold, He tears down, and it cannot be rebuilt; He imprisons a man, and there can be no release. Behold, He restrains the waters, and they dry up; And He sends them out, and they inundate the earth. With Him are strength and sound wisdom,*
>
> *The misled and the misleader belong to Him. He makes counselors walk barefoot and makes fools of judges. He loosens the bond of kings. And binds their loins with a girdle. He makes priests walk barefoot and overthrows the secure ones. He deprives the trusted ones of speech. And takes away the discernment of the elders. He pours contempt on nobles. And loosens the belt of the strong.*
>
> *He reveals mysteries from the darkness. And brings the deep darkness into light. He makes the nations great, then destroys them; He enlarges the nations, then leads them away. He deprives of intelligence the chiefs of the earth's people and makes them wander in a pathless waste. They*

grope in darkness with no light, and He makes them stagger like a drunken man." [25]

I am amazed at the Lord. He has just filled my mouth with the words from Job 12, words I have never read before and I realize that He is teaching me as He teaches this mix of men.

One by one, I take a prisoner by the arm to his own interrogation room. Each blindly feels for the table and chair as I tell him to sit. There are fifteen rooms each with a Jihadi leader sitting in it. The eighteen that remain are sitting on the floor in a hallway guarded by angels. All are waiting for what they believe they deserve. Each is sweating, fearing the tools of torture: hammers, pliers, lighters, water, battery cables and long knives. Each is remembering times when they have been the interrogators and are imagining what will be done to them out of their memories of what they have done to others. Twenty-four of these men are feeling guilty. Nine of them are angry that anyone would question them and dare to invade a private meeting of all the Jihadi leadership in this region of Syria.

I leave each in his state of blindness and fear, in perfect silence, quietly closing their doors behind me. Let each of them dwell on what will be done to them and what they have done to others. They are beginning to hear the blood cry out from the ground on each of the ones they have tortured and murders they have ordered or committed for Allah. They think about the mere men who are in control. These are men who kill for the sheer enjoyment of the action itself and the fear it creates, the ones who run to do evil.

Those who are feeling the guilt and shame, the uncertainty of their brand of righteousness, and the conviction of sin are beginning to say, "I'm sorry, Lord. Do with me what you will. I can never repay what I have stolen in lives and in the peace of those I have hurt."

Jesus speaks to each of them, one on one, and identifies Himself. With those who are repentant, reverential and submissive, He is gentle. For those who are rebellious, defiant, and raging, He is firm and uncompromising.

"I am Jesus of Nazareth whom you persecute. I came to this Earth that you might live, and you have mocked, tortured, raped and murdered without mercy. You will receive 100-fold what you have meted out to the innocents under your control."

Those who are repentant are given food and water and a bed for the night. It will be three days before their sight is restored, and in that time, I will tell them about their new King. The angels will minister to them, as Heirs of Salvation. The sounds of their violent memories are quieted, and peace surrounds them. They are not slaves. They can leave at any time, but these have met Jesus face to face and are not going anywhere apart from Him. They all are receiving a download of Who He is, and each has heard the Great Commission directly from His lips. They are all to teach, minister to, and care for the sheep—those who are already Christians, and those unfortunates, especially the moderate Muslims and Yazidi in their paths who desire to know Him.

Those who remain rebellious and shake their fist at Him are taken to another room—a prison cell—where they will reside together. Their meals will be bread and water. They will sleep on the floor and share the same bathroom bucket. As I take them to their cell surrounded by heavy angelic guard, I see a dark shadow that moves and expands with the appearance of black chiffon descending over their faces. It grows until it surrounds and encompasses their whole body, causing the appearance of each to disappear in a dark shadow. An 11-foot angel, dressed in full battle gear, will guard them until the remaining 33 days are over and the trumpet blows. At that time, the angel will be called back to HQ—Heaven—and the inmates will be freed at the whim of the next guard.

I remain until each of the 24 repentant men receives his sight. Each of them looks at me with tears in their eyes, humble and radiant with the light and glory of the Lord. Each hug me and thanks me for the Truth, for mercy, compassion and grace. Each realizes that he didn't get what he deserved, which was violent punishment. He received grace instead. Each man has an angel assigned to him that will remain with him in the physical realm. That angel will protect, encourage and minister to him so each of their assignments is fulfilled for as long as they shall be on the earth. The knowledge that this has happened in all twelve regions within Syria amazes me.

As I turn to leave, the spirits Doubt and Scorn return. They remind me of my choice to turn away, implying that once my choice is made, there is no grace to change my mind. I don't answer to them. I answer only to the Lord and it is here that I look up to Heaven and make my vow to love Him for all eternity and declare Him the Lord of my life. It is here that I forgive my parents and any that contributed to the hardships I faced as a young adult man who had moved from a tightly sheltered missionary life in southern Africa to a first world city in Amsterdam, the Netherlands, where everything was new and nothing was familiar.

I put the refractor in my pocket as I walk out of the burned-out building, passing through the doorway. I find myself coming out of the coffee house in Amsterdam, wallet in hand, back to my bike. It has been a glorious "day".

Bennett talks to me as I walk my bike home, "Because of you twelve and your obedience to the Lord, there are 350 leaders who have come to the Lord. Each of these will convert at least 60% of their subordinates and care for those they previously committed to destroy. All Yazidi in the region will be saved, 14,440 in number. 84% of Muslims in Syria will also be converted to Jesus, the Merciful King.

You have done well, Thomas. Welcome back to the fold. Do you have any questions about this assignment or the overall mission?"

I respond. "I have no questions about the assignment or the mission. I do have one question though."

"What is it?" he asks.

"If there is no sickness or infirmity or disability in Heaven, why are you wearing glasses?" I respond.

"Good question, Thomas. You are right in saying that there is no need for glasses in Heaven, but these help me to see through the darkness on earth. The time is short, and the atmosphere is getting darker every day. Soon, but not yet, there will be a time when Light will reign for 1,000 years and then they can be retired permanently," he says with a grin.

CHAPTER 11

THE DARK NET AND ADAN'S VORTEX

DAY 12, SATURDAY, AUGUST 22 – T MINUS 28
ARIELLE CHEVALIER
AVIGNON, FRANCE & SYDNEY, AUSTRALIA

ANDEL LASKA
PRAGUE, CZECHOSLOVAKIA

ISABELLA OBSERVES:

I am standing in the War Room of Heaven watching a live 3D hologram of time and space. I am observing both Arielle and Andel in their assigned operations for tonight. Curiously, only one has GPS latitude and longitudinal coordinates. One is working in a "real" place, the other, a virtual one.

ARIELLE:

I have been at work since noon today. I was called in early by my nursing supervisor. Today is Saturday and my work cohorts tend to call off sick on the weekends, leaving the Intensive Care Unit where I work dangerously short staffed. It is now 11:45p.m. and I should have gone home fifteen minutes ago but I am still hard at work finishing my charting in the hospital computer's electronic medical records system.

It's late and I am tired. The unit is quiet except for the bleeping of monitors and the hum of ventilators. It is at these times that I have the time to think and remember who I am and the call of God on my life. My name is Arielle Chevalier and my name means "Lion of God". My surname, Chevalier, means "Knight" and it is prophetic, as I am a Knight in the Army of God. I am thirty-six, born in Avignon, France and currently living in Sydney, Australia.

Avignon has a religious heritage, known historically as the French Vatican. In the 14th Century, during the years between 1309 and 1377, there were seven successive popes that resided in the city. Avignon was officially purchased in 1348 by Pope Clement VI and remained the papal "seat" until the late 1700's when it was handed to France during the French Revolution.

The spirit of Religion remains there to this day, though it is considerably weaker than when the papacy was officially located in Avignon. That spirit, and the one that filled Joan of Arc which included wisdom, prophecy, courage and leadership, are the ones I lived under for the first twenty-five years of my life. That was when I met my then husband-to-be, an American physician finishing his residency in France, who convinced me to marry him and move to Australia.

Married for eight years, my husband Scott and I have three children, all under the age of six. I work part time as a nurse in the ICU, 24 hours a week, at a large hospital in Sydney. To say that my life is busy is an understatement. The one thing that gives me enormous energy is the daily assignments I have enjoyed the past couple of weeks. The places I have been and the people whose lives I have touched have created new life in me. I have told Scott about the portal, the first night on the mountain with all of the others that share the calling, and some of the specific missions, but it is difficult for him to share in my excitement or even believe in the plausibility of it. This great work is a very big secret with only 144 people and their angels aware of what we are doing.

I put the finishing touches on my Nursing Notes and begin to sign off, which will shut down the computer in my patient's room, when I hear Bennett's voice say two short words: *"Dark Net"*.

I can see my puzzled reflection in the screen monitor and though I have not moved a millimeter closer, I see my reflection growing, little by little, as if my face is only inches from it. I am discerning that this time the portal to my mission is my computer itself and I feel the slight transformation as I "shrink" from my natural age of 36 to 33 years old.

In a nanosecond I am inside the screen, as are my angels, Gabriella and Paul. We descend from all that is familiar, productive and light into what can only be classified as the dungeon of the Internet. The portion of the Internet and the applications that I encounter on a short-term daily basis are functional and fruitful but, like the tip of an iceberg, what is seen is only a fraction of what exists.

I move from above the "water's surface" of the Net to the much larger, deeper and darker "Dark Net" through the computer's physical and virtual infrastructure. Suddenly, it is as if I am a tiny corpuscle in the circulatory system of a 220-pound man, moving along the voltages in electronic circuits, in bits and bytes via routers, into and out of memory, through fiber-optic cables, into a huge cavern of blackness.

ISABELLA LOOKS TO ANOTHER OF THE SPECIAL FORCES:

Across the world in San Francisco, California, I observe the beginnings of another Special Forces Ops, this one led by Andel Laska. Even watching puts me in a state of suspense until I remember under Whose orders this mission is truly controlled. Each Troop is equipped for the mission, each angel given strict orders of protection. Still, the determination in Andel is contagious.

ANDEL:

I am awake already, feeling a sense of urgency even in my sleep. My dreams about clock works and hourglasses and the darkness encroaching on my day run around in my head, as I lay in bed, restless. It is 11:59 p.m. and I look over and watch the next minute roll over to midnight.

A portal opens suddenly as if time can no longer wait for me and I am sucked violently through it. I can feel the Lord's urgency as the hour is fast approaching when the lost will be lost for eternity. The Word says that all of Heaven rejoices when one lost sheep is found and that the Father waits and watches for his prodigals to come home.

I land on a dark street. It is 1:30 in the morning and we find ourselves walking toward our destination in the city known to have the stronghold of Sodom. As Elsa, Jacob, Rebekah, and I walk into the darkness, suddenly we are being fired at by balls of fire from the sky. It is as if the old brick streets are being blown apart and what is left is melting away. Roots like hands are coming up from the ground to grab our ankles. Doors and windows of the buildings we pass open and change shape, stretching out their hands to try to hold us back. We have not felt this much resistance in any of our assignments so far. It is as if the very structures and infrastructure of the city is in league with the Devil himself over our mission's target tonight.

There are creatures that are half bird and half dragon, like the gargoyles that sit on the rooftops of some people's homes for "luck", swooping down on us. One of them struck my helmet aiming for my right eye. I think to myself that the person this one fights for is not lucky at all.

Men on the street are darkly hollow-eyed, staring at us in hatred with invisible gargoyles on their shoulders. Some of them attempt to stand in our path but they quickly move aside with fear in their eyes, the closer we get to them.

We are walking downhill and have only walked two blocks, six more to go. We feel the electric charge in the air, a bit like the feel of the anointing, only *this* anointing is the epitome of evil and it is pushing back at us, trying to keep us from advancing. We hear the beat of techno dance music, the sound of raucous laughter and the shrieks of madness.

All through the missions of the past few days I have walked, flown, been blown through or sucked through heavenly portals in strategic places all over the earth. Traveling down the remaining six blocks of this street I will reach a different kind of portal. It is a place where the deceived meet the rebellious. It is a place where the vulnerable make the acquaintance of the tares sown by the enemy. It is the Devil's attempt to damn a category of mankind made in the image of God. I am approaching a vortex of Hell where the king of Sodom himself is holding court tonight.

ISABELLA COMMENTS:

The virtual atmosphere of the Dark Net is no less dangerous, insidious or malicious. Knowing the relentlessness of hackers and computer architects who run to do evil from their computer monitors, tracing with evil eyes the movements of holy invaders, changes the assignments of Arielle's angels from warring with swords or lazars to providing a shield of invisibility. I whisper a prayer of protection.

ARIELLE:

The dark and murky cavern is where I end up, which now resembles a huge palace in a kingdom of darkness, a dark manor home with hundreds of rooms on the inside, all without windows for light. The rooms comprise everything from emails and IRS files and medical records to the "offices" of hackers and thieves. Rooms where everything from demographic, financial and medical data is held, to those containing weapons, people, and sex, for sale. There are porn and pedophilia chat rooms and message boards that are separated by "walls" that delineate topics.

These rooms are accessed via back door programs created and entered by superior hackers to be used by governments, psychopaths, mob bosses and drug lords in order to control those whose records they contain. Vulnerabilities of the rich, famous, poor and ordinary are exploited. The ones who exploit are anarchists, loyal only to themselves or those like them. It has made gangs, Russian mafia, criminals and those with evil intent extremely wealthy as it has stolen the secrets, bodies and lives of their victims. Access is like an octopus, entering through relatively innocuous information and moving to the most private and delicate secrets possessed by the individual. The information it inhabits is used for extortion and blackmail until the person pays or dies. Lives are lost. People are tortured and brutalized. Wives and daughters raped. Children sold into a life of servitude or sexual slavery.

And there is no one to save.

Bennett brings to my remembrance a childhood movie about mermaids who make deals with a sea witch who promises them anything they want if only they pay what cannot be paid. The victims are sea urchins, hopeless souls without bodies, living in chains and the prisons of vows that can't be kept, owing *themselves* forevermore. The sea witch is a picture of Satan. The prison, a picture of Hell, and the souls are those that will be kept there for eternity.

They are my Targets tonight. This is evil on a scale that I have never encountered personally before and I admit that I feel a twinge of fear. The enemy is sitting on a throne in the center of the large hall inside the "manor home" within the cavern. He smiles a twisted grimace of a smile and sees my fear as a slit in my armor that will allow him entry. He is sadly mistaken as I remember the words of the Lord reiterated by the angel on the very first night. *There is no way that I can fail.* I trust in the Lord.

Isabella continues to watch from the monitors of the War Room.

ANDEL:

Suddenly we are filled with the Holy Spirit's power and receive the strength we need to continue our short walk. The stronghold over this part of the city is ancient satanic witchcraft, occult, perversion, fear, and murder, but all over the skies and street surrounding this part of town are the heavenly host, many of whom I recognize from previous battles. This battle has already been won in the heavenlies.

The target is a nineteen-year-old boy named Adan. The name "Adan" means "man" and his manhood is what is being fought over. Although his soul is in no real danger, I am here for his destiny, his call and his purpose on this Earth and for those whose lives he will touch.

We are in San Francisco, California and the year is 1987. I receive a download of information beginning 34 weeks before Adan is born. I see his mother, a sixteen-year-old high school student and his father, an eighteen-year-old football player. I see the family conflict. His mother comes from an affluent socially connected family, and they do not want the scandal associated with a grandchild born out of wedlock. She fights them and they turn their anger on her, insisting she abort her baby. They send her to a counseling agency where instead of being advised by a woman, she receives pregnancy counseling by two flamboyant, gay men. She finally agrees to the abortion, feeling she has no choice.

As she sits on the abortion table sobbing, the doctor decides he will not go against her will just to placate her parents and grandparents, though they all socialize in the same circles. He sends her home with prenatal vitamins instead. Her mother yells, "I hope you have a girl that brings the same shame on your head as you have brought on mine!"

What her mother doesn't know is that the seed life she carries is that of a boy. And he is already planted in her womb.

She and the baby's father try to work things out, but she is young and immature, and he is resentful. They split up after two months. Adan is born a beautiful baby boy, but curses had been spoken over him before his birth by people who did not understand the power of their words. He feels same sex attraction that began at the age of four in some of his earliest memories.

His mother later married a nice and kind "man's man" with whom Adan has little in common. His interests run counter to his stepfather's.

He feels no man has ever claimed him as his own in a fatherly role. He begins to experiment in drama, drugs, and sexual fantasy.

Adan's aunt is a believer and she leads him to the Lord at seventeen years old but the urgings in his soul are persuasive. He comes out a gay man nine months after accepting Christ. He parties and uses ecstasy regularly. The drugs make him feel warm and accepted into the gay community—his new family. But the Lord is talking to him, gradually convicting him to change his life and renounce the path he has been on. He breaks up with his lover and tells some of his friends of his decision. He does not discern the change in them as he talks. He does not see the vertical pupil in their eyes and the serpent's blink.

Two of his friends, a woman and a man, talk him into one last evening at the bars where he is well known. His friends loan him a yellow satin jacket, an oversized baseball cap with a question mark on it, orange leopard sunglasses and platform shoes to complete the outfit. As he leaves the house, he hears the voice of God ask him if he is a fool; yellow means warning, the question mark means he is clueless, and he looks like a fool. Adan has been warned by the Holy Spirit not to leave his home, but he goes out to the bars anyway. He promises himself that this is the last time.

The female friend who invited Adan out tried to tell his fortune in the past. She says she "dabbles" in witchcraft. The reality is that she has seen by the spirit of Lucifer that Adan is now a believer. She considers him dangerous now and decides he must be dealt with. She makes her plans as they enter the club.

ISABELLA:

As I watch Arielle's progress, I have always felt uneasy at the thought of victims who are not allowed to defend themselves. The virtual environment allows multiple victims, unrelated, in different geographical locations, some guilty and some innocent, all from the comfort of a desk chair or filthy couch in a basement apartment.

ARIELLE:

Suddenly, a blue light begins to blink, and a tracer camera starts to follow me with its tiny eye. Gabriella and Paul surround me, or rather, what has identified me as an intruder. If we were on the street, they would grow to their double-digit angelic heights, but in this virtual place they are what appears to be transparent. As they surround me, I am like a chameleon, invisible to whatever has started tracking me. Nothing to see here, folks!

Bennett begins to identify those that I have been calling indentured sea urchins that are assigned to me: "There are sixteen children being used in a pedophile ring, ages six to fifteen, including two from Bangkok, one from Ukraine, one from Idaho, one from Sweden, two from Central America, two from Mexico and one from Berlin. There are four young women from Estonia and Russia, and two 14-year-old boys from New York, both of them runaways from the foster system. The sex slave trade is extremely lucrative in that the 'product' can be bought and paid for many times all day, every day. The perverted appetites of the ones who purchase these services are insatiable in the evil days on Earth at this time in its history. Extreme darkness has prevailed until now, but the end is in sight.

Also, in the folder is information about a drug dealer from Mexico, along with his parents and four sisters. The owner of the file believes the dealer has betrayed him by embezzling thousands of dollars and put a contract out on him and his family to be punished by rape, torture and murder. The file owner is setting a precedent and making an example of them, wanting to make sure that no one dares to betray them again. A deal with two contractors is pending now.

Finally, there are also a banker from Switzerland, a jeweler from London and a school custodian in Ontario, Canada, all being blackmailed for sexual indiscretions and living in terror of losing everything and having those discretions come to the light to their loved ones."

It is interesting to me that the folder I see is three-dimensional and the records within it having real faces. Also interesting is that most of the file involves sex trafficking and slavery, but others contained within the same folder are in unrelated industries. The only thing that they all have in common is that they have cried out to God for help and He has heard them.

Bennett continues, "We have others of the Special Forces assigned to these same people all over the earth to take over the evacuation of the victims. Your job is to delete their files so that there will be no audit trail. As they are wiped from the memory of the Dark Net, they will be wiped from the memory of the transgressors and the subcontractors as well. No one will know to look for them and no one will be accused of betraying the thugs, pimps and crime bosses. There will be no need for witness protection. All of them will see the mercy of the One who has set them free and will feel the freedom today on Earth and forever in eternity. Perfect Love has cast out fear! They will be used as instruments in God's hands to rescue, rehabilitate, comfort and evangelize Jesus Christ and the Kingdom from this point forward to all who will listen to them.

There are sixteen Light Ops Special Forces and Angelic troops tonight deployed to five continents and thirteen countries to rescue all of them. It's later than it has ever been, but in spite of the lateness of time in the history of man, there will be over three thousand saved before the great and terrible day of the Lord. As the pressure in the funnel of the end of days increases, acceleration and multiplication will increase in salvations as well."

I don't have a delete button to push on a computer console. All I see is symbolism—circuits, electricity, tunnels of cables and file folders. The folders are individual areas like rooms separated by transparent walls with a gate as a doorway. The gate is the symbolism for a door that, when opened will empty the folder.

I walk in the darkness to each of their gates and open it. Each of the "urchins" passes through the door and promptly vaporizes. They are no longer prisoners and their histories are obliterated without a trace, a permanent deletion of data that can never be restored. The Special Forces on the surface of the earth are all in their places, offering solace and solutions for the destined future of each of the saved. Not one of them is lost. With grateful hearts, they are servants of the Lord for the remainder of their lives. These are willing servants of the King, no longer held against their will.

The last gate is opened, and the captives are freed. My assignment is complete. In the blink of an eye I am in the room of my last patient. Five minutes have passed, and my computer is in sleep mode, which is where I need to be. I clock out and am translated home within thirty seconds. I find myself giggling that instant destinations are one of the rewards of these assignments, a perk of the job. I lay down next to my husband and whisper a prayer of thanks that I was chosen so long ago to be an instrument in the freedom and destiny of others.

Isabella watches, continuing to pray in the Spirit.

ANDEL:

Tonight, Adan has taken the last dose of Ecstasy that he will ever take, hoping for the same love, acceptance, and warmth that he has come to expect. Instead he feels a surge of fear. He hears the voices of accusing spirits. Adan tries to leave the club, knowing he has made a dreadful mistake, but a handsome, mysterious and spiritually dark stranger stands in the shadows directly in his path.

Adan runs and stumbles, falling to his knees. He is terrified. The stranger steps out of the darkness and gives him a knowing look. He slowly shakes his head from side to side as if to say "You're not going anywhere. You won't escape."

The stranger is the owner of the club and Adan recognizes him. He calls himself "B-Z" and only a select few know that the nickname is short for Beelzebub. Adan is hallucinating in fear. He sees an innocent looking, very pale toddler, walk up to him in this dark, musically throbbing nightclub. The child's mouth opens, and he speaks in an adult man's very deep gravelly voice. He asks, "Where is your God now?"

The woman, his "friend", does more than dabble in witchcraft. She is the highest witch in a coven in Northern California and he is genuinely afraid. She tells him he can check in anytime he likes, but he can never leave. And she means it. They are setting legal precedent in the demonic spirit world. Adan is a believer. If he is murdered tonight as she has promised him, he will be at the command of B-Z, he will be in Heaven for eternity, but the enemy will have the earthly victory. The enemy will attempt to justify an eternal sentence in Hell related to Adan's lifestyle through legalistic accusations to the Father Himself. The evil stranger is the king of Sodom, the Devil incarnate, and has given the order for Adan's execution.

It is, however, not God's plan that Adan should die tonight. The Holy Spirit speaks into Adan's spirit to show no fear. If he shows the fear they are hungry to see, he will surely die.

I feel the darkness grow the closer we get to the club where Adan is trying to hide. Demons with evil smiles and elongated eyes as if made up with theatre make up, are standing in our path. They are rubbing up against Jacob and me, only to skitter off in terror as they are knocked out of the way. This is my assignment and I feel no fear. I am in the right place at the right time.

The demonic and satanic presence and pressure is attempting to push us away from the entrance. It's like being blown by a strong wind. The smell is sickeningly sweet as if trying to hide something dead and rotting. The music is relentless, pounding and very loud. Without the distraction of it, a person might have second thoughts about being there. The heavy darkness in the club feels as though the light is *unable* to shine. There are colored lights pulsing on the dance floor and I can see bodies against bodies and all of them male. They are a single mass of limbs, moving to the beat of the music.

I have not yet seen Adan but suddenly I feel pulled to the back room of the club. I am drawn down a dark and narrow hallway that leads to restrooms, storage rooms and an office. There are other doors in the hallway, and I can only imagine their purpose.

I walk through the entrance of a large office with a huge desk. There is a truly ugly, disfigured man dressed all in black sitting near it in an overstuffed armchair. He is caught unaware by my presence but when he sees me, he instantly transforms himself into the handsome stranger that had been on the dance floor just minutes ago. He is Beelzebub himself. Pride has always been one of his issues. And for one created so beautiful, he now must hide his hideous form due to the sin he introduced to the world so long ago. He is quite angry at the sight of me and recognizes that I am one of the Lord's army. He seems to know that I am there for Adan.

Adan's "friend," the high priestess of witchcraft, is sitting at the desk as well. She has curved knives and carving instruments on the desk in front of her that look ancient. They have been used for two hundred years, passed down from high priestess to high priestess in this part of California. They are used specifically for ritual sacrifice and punitive executions. Since Adan is a believer, his will be both a sacrifice to the Devil and execution as punishment. She is greedy for blood. Her excitement is building, and she feeds off the fear of her victims. As I walk in, she discerns that I am not there to revel in witchcraft, the occult or Devil worship. She stupidly thinks that there might be two people sacrificed tonight.

At the back of the room is another pair of armchairs. Seated in one of them is a frightened Adan, but he is strengthened moment by moment because of the One sitting in the chair next to his. Though he sees no one there, he senses the presence of Jesus.

B-Z follows my eyes and sees Jesus. His eyes fleetingly show his fear, but he quickly recovers, and his fury is immediate.

Jesus calmly looks at B-Z and the Devil begins to sweat profusely, nervously licking his lips with a forked tongue. The witch wonders what is happening, as she cannot see everyone in the room. Her mood changes from excitement and anticipation to anxiety as she sees B-Z's loss of control. She can smell the fear on him.

Jesus calmly looks at B-Z and a smile is forming on His lips. He states clearly, "*You have already lost the war, and you have lost this battle as well. Adan is Mine. Release him and let him go.*"

B-Z is angry, but he remembers his own humiliation on that Good Friday two millennia ago when he was bound in chains, naked and led through all of the chambers of Hell as he was paraded in victory by the Man sitting before him now. B-Z doesn't like to lose even one soul, but it is not worth another potential humiliation in front of both men and demons tonight. The only consequence of letting Adan go will be that the witch who worships B-Z will be a witness to Adan's departure without even a fight.

I escort Adan out of the club through the men he has befriended and loved. His love for them is tangible and many stop dancing and talking to each other to watch him depart. They know they will not see him in this place again. Some of them have envy on their faces as they sense the chains, they themselves are wearing. Many of those will seek him out in the future to find for themselves what has changed him. I lead Adan to the next place in his life's journey, which is a place for his continued healing and rehabilitation. He is joyful and humble, and his servant's heart will give him the reward of many crowns in his future. And then Jesus says audibly the words Adan longed to hear his entire life: *"Adan is My son."*

As I leave him, the Lord appears and walks at my side.

"The call I have on Adan's life is a big one and one that the enemy matched in temptation, deception and tribulation. His desire is only to kill, steal and destroy. He came close with Adan, but Adan's redemption is complete. I have an awesome plan and a future for him. He will lead many out of darkness and restore hope to those who thought their hope was gone forever. Old things are wiped away. I make all things new again.

Adan will marry a beautiful woman who belongs to Me and together their destiny will be achieved. I will continue to cover and protect him because the enemy hates redemption. Many in the world will say that there is a gay gene. They will say that a gay man can't be delivered, healed, or changed and there will be threats to his and his family's lives. Adan will respond to the growing issue of identity and whether a person is born into it or assumes it by choice. There will be many who are comforted and brought to wholeness through him."

Elsa, Jacob and Rebekah walk me to a portal in a coffee shop where I am instantly returned to my bed. It is 1:10 a.m. on the night I left home, but I have been "gone" two full days.

Bennett and Isabella: "Excellent job Andel and Arielle!"

Arielle replies, "Can we do it again tomorrow?"

Andel grins and agrees. "Roger that!"

CHAPTER 12
KATHLEEN MARY MCDONALD

DAY 15, TUESDAY, AUGUST 25 -T MINUS 25
PRISCILLA GRAHAM
AUCKLAND, AUSTRALIA

ISABELLA:

Priscilla is newly widowed. Her husband, Jim was her dearest friend and they had looked forward to twenty or thirty more years together when he was taken home to be with the Lord soon after retiring. She has felt betrayed in her abandonment, alone, unnecessary and hopeless until the night on the mountain when everything changed.

Priscilla awakens slowly in her bed and realizes that she slept all night with dreams of Heaven and Hell. She tossed and turned as darkness encroaches in her dreams and she slept in perfect peace with a smile on her face, laughing once or twice in her sleep. She has seen how the enemy of her soul hates the people of God and the people without God, too. Just as God has a plan and a purpose for us, so too does the Devil.

Today she is curious as to what the day and her assignment holds for her.

PRISCILLA:

It is Sunday morning and I rise to get myself ready for church. There is a missionary coming as a guest speaker this morning and I consider this with fresh eyes. Whereas before I might have dozed off or let my mind wander in different directions when people visited from places across the world, today I eagerly anticipate what I will hear. They are messengers to the Kingdom as am I, and I can't wait to meet them.

Praise and worship are glorious and all who are there enter into the Presence of God. As we sit to hear the message, a young man of about twenty-five is introduced. He speaks with a Scottish brogue and I consider my own roots. I am one-third Scottish, one-third Irish, and one-third English myself. Once again, my eyes begin to close as I imagine the places of my own ancestry.

Suddenly I am transported to London, England, literally in two places at one time. The year is 1915, early in the month of January. Unlike other assignments, this time I am a witness to history that has already taken place, a passive observer. I watch the scenes as if I am at ceiling height and invisible to those who are living in them. I am transported within this history, from window to window, seeing what has been, and glimpsing what must be redeemed. Unlike Ebenezer Scrooge, in Charles Dickens' *A Christmas Carol*, I am witnessing a life without myself in it. I am able to walk amongst those in the scene without being seen, as he did.

I see a young Scottish woman, Kathleen Mary McDonald, who has just arrived in London from her home near Edinburgh, Scotland in 1915. Her face is lovely. Her eyes a beautiful shade of green, and she has a small mark, like a strawberry, high on her right cheekbone.

The home she comes to is one of three throughout England that is owned by the same family. It is large and grand, and she is more than a little intimidated. She is to be a governess of the family's three small children and this is her first position. Kathleen is young, sixteen, and has been deployed as a governess because of her own family's lack of resources, but she is educated, wise, and innocent. She can be a friend, a teacher, a playmate, and a mother to the children to whom she will be assigned. She knocks on the door and a middle-aged butler answers, his face is stern and "correct", but his eyes twinkle. She meets with the woman of the home and later, her husband. Finally, she meets her new young wards and the rapport that is established is immediate. She is shown to her new room.

I continue on and witness the next frame.

Kathleen is happy in her position, though she misses her mother, father, two sisters and brother who remain home in Scotland. The young family loves her and the children she cares for are thriving under her attention. Nearly a year passes and Christmas Eve approaches. The family is planning a large party for the holidays and guests will come from all over England.

The day arrives and is filled with merriment. Food and drink abound. By nine-thirty that evening, the children are tired and one or two of the guests are showing their liquor intake. She gets the children into bed and closes the door to their three-bedroom suite. She turns to go to her own room and runs into her master's younger brother—a twenty-five-year-old boy who has had too much to drink. He has played with the family's wealth and has been a rogue, wild with women—both friends and those of ill repute. Early in the day he set his eyes on Kathleen. She has been uncomfortable in his presence for much of the day, as he has watched her as a predator watches his prey. She has looked forward to putting her charges into bed and retiring herself. But such is not to be the case.

He is too close. His smile lazy, and his eyes dangerous. She backs away but he is getting closer and closer until his hands are around her waist. She sees that she is on a precipice and her life, as she knows it, is about to change forever through no fault of her own. She opens her mouth to scream and his hand covers her mouth. He tells her how beautiful she is and half pushes, half drags her down the hall to an empty room. She begs him to stop but her cries are muffled. She hears the party music and laughter in the other part of the house, but no one can hear her. Through her physical pain she feels emotional agony.

And then he is finished.

As he buttons his trousers and combs his hair with his fingers, he looks down on her, still trying to keep herself covered. His eyes reveal his feelings as he travels through triumph, then regret, pity, and finally fear. He knows she was a virgin and that he has caused her pain, both to her body and to her mind. He fears the wrath of his brother and sister-in-law and hopes they will never know. He backs out of the room, both sorry for his actions and angry because she is only a servant and not worth his remorse.

The following day is Christmas. The children are excited and can hardly wait to get to the family study where a large tree stands in front of the window, underneath filled with presents. Kathleen, normally joyful, calm, and impeccable is dull. Her hair is mussed and her lace cap slightly askew. Her uniform is in place, but it is as if her world has tilted and she has not compensated for it. The children's mother notices and looks at Kathleen with concern. She asks if she feels all right, but Kathleen cannot meet her eyes. Kathleen says that she is fine, but her eyes are filled with tears. She tries to smile brightly, making the excuse that she is homesick for her family at Christmas. She gets down on the floor to play with the children and turns her face away, now pink to the roots of her red hair. She does not see the look that passes from the mistress of the house to her husband. They had witnessed the unwanted attention during the day from his brother, suspecting that he might try to get her alone. And as an admission of guilt, he left at first light on Christmas morning.

The next window frames Kathleen two months later, early in the morning as she struggles to rise from an exhausted sleep. She looks sick, gray from nausea, and vomits into her chamber pot. Her monthly time did not come and has revealed, combined with her morning sickness, that she became pregnant during the Christmas Eve rape. She feels that, while no one knows her secret now, in a few short months she will no longer be able to hide it and her disgrace will be revealed. She is mortified at the shame of it. She has caught the eyes of the women servants of the house. The concern in her mistress' eyes shows that they are beginning to suspect they know the truth about her situation. She is ashamed and knows that she must do something. If things go on the way of nature, her attack will be known but she will reap the consequences. She will lose her job, be sent home, and bring shame to herself and to her family. How will she live through it?

She drags herself up, washes her face and teeth, brushes her hair and puts it neatly into a bun. Finally, she is dressed and ready for the day. Another wave of nausea threatens to overtake her as she makes her way to the servant's kitchen to get something into her stomach. She navigates her way down the stairs just in time to wretch into a large bowl. She is fortunate that only a single cook has witnessed her sickness, but the cook's eyes are filled with awareness as to the cause of it. Kathleen dumps the bowl and washes it thoroughly. She reaches for a piece of bread to stave off the nausea. The cook comes to her and drapes a loving arm around her shoulders, eyes filled with compassion and knowing. She fixes Kathleen a cup of tea and sits her down to rest and to have a talk, one that Kathleen knows is coming and dreads. Her secret is out to one person and with relief she pours out the truth of the situation.

In the next window of time, Priscilla watches Kathleen walking on one of the seedier streets in the city of London. She has been driven to the city by the family car under the pretense of shopping for the children. She makes her way on foot to a seedier part of town to a dark doorway, her face blotchy with tears and her eyes showing her hopelessness. The small sign outside the door reads "Thelonius Porter, MD". The doorway leads to a small vestibule where she takes off her hat and waits. After a quarter of an hour, a middle-aged man comes into the room. He is wearing a brown suit, jacket removed, and an apron over a white shirt, sleeves rolled up. He looks at her with compassion, but he knows the sooner they do what she has come to do, the sooner her life will get back on course. He takes her back to his exam room and the door closes.

In the next frame, I see Kathleen back at home in her bed. She has told the family that she is not feeling well, and her face reveals the truth of that statement. She is very pale and holds her stomach as if it pains her. She has two high spots of pink on her face and the little strawberry mark on her right cheek seems to melt into it. The mistress of the houses comes to her room and sits on the side of the bed. Her eyes are filled with compassion and guilt. She has spoken to the cook, who has also seen Kathleen and knows that something is amiss. The cook pours out the story, keeping nothing back, including her recommendation of the doctor in London.

As Kathleen looks at her mistress, she realizes that she can no longer feel shame or fear. She is struggling to lift her head. Breathing is hard. The mistress turns back the covers to see and the bed is filled with blood.

She runs to the door to cry for help but within an hour, Kathleen is dead. She has bled to death.

The next two frames in time are six months later. The first shows the household in sorrow and failing to thrive. Kathleen's loss hit the children and the mother very hard, but the master of the house is affected as well, as are the servants. It is a tragedy that the incident with the master's brother happened at all, but the real heartbreak was the botched abortion. Though they have received spiritual counseling from the family's minister, there seems to be no comfort. They cannot even pray. Can the dead be brought to life again?

The doctor, Thelonius Porter, MD, had been a reputable physician with two practices and two offices, the latter to "help" women for a price. Society does not approve, though they believe his services necessary. For this "service" his office is in a less desirable location and one where his regular highbrow patients cannot witness the reality of it.

The second frame shows the doctor himself. He had seen Kathleen's emotional distress over the decision and pressured her to go through with it. Over the years, his heart had grown unsympathetic. How many mistakes would he have to fix? Now, however, he has faced devastating consequences through Kathleen's employers in the form of loss to his reputation. His conscience bothers him constantly and he is tormented by the memory of her cries. He has begun to drink to silence the voices in his head. His patients are leaving in droves. His wife is ashamed of him and has left him to live across town with her sister. He has lost everything that ever mattered to him. He contemplates suicide because he feels he cannot live with himself.

It is here that time stops. I know my assignment is one of redemption, but it is obvious that I am too late. "Lord?"

The Lord begins to speak,

"Her destiny was a great one, motherhood, evangelism and a teaching ministry on the continents of Africa and Asia with her husband. She had a legacy to pass down to her children. She chose Me before the foundation of the Earth, even as I chose her. I would have used her situation to prosper much of the world, but she was filled with fear, shame, and self-loathing, as if she were to blame. Her path has changed and that has affected the destiny of hundreds of thousands. My plan for her is good and she will adore the daughter she carried. Even the stars are crying out for her destiny to be realized. That is why you are here, victorious one."

Suddenly I am no longer a witness to the movie frames I have been watching of Kathleen's life and, in fact, the movie has been rewound to the point at which Kathleen is dropped off in the city.

I find myself in the seedy neighborhood where the doctor's office is. I am not witnessing the situation outside of reality but am in the situation, as are my angels, Max and Micah, with feet on the ground. Although neither could ever see it this way, Kathleen Mary McDonald and Dr. Thelonius Porter have a divine appointment today. This day will change the course of their futures and redeem a past that is out of alignment with God's plan for their lives. No longer will one cause, deliberately or accidentally, the death of others, including the unborn. No longer will the other run in fear, but rather welcome the challenges life has to offer, along with all its joy.

Kathleen is a block from me and is moving in my direction. Her head is bowed, and her shoulders are slumped as if she carries the weight of the world on them. She looks up and meets my eyes. There is a shock of recognition, though of course we have never met. She quickly looks away and enters a storefront dry goods market. She is hiding. After a few minutes she exits the store and turns in the other direction away from Dr. Porter's office.

The street is narrow and dirty, the neighborhood poor. The alleyways are narrower still, with clotheslines connecting one apartment building to another. Women stand in the doorways; some are gossiping with neighbors, and others selling their wares. Poor and ragged children are visible to both Kathleen and me, even as they are invisible in the society of which they are unfortunate members. There is a fine smoke mixing with light fog hovering at roof height. The smell of garbage and the smoke from garbage burning represents the familiar smell of poverty to those who live there. The alley feels like a tall box with four-story, dark brown brick buildings on both sides and covered by a hazy ceiling. The box traps the inhabitants in a prison and chains them there for life.

My assignment is to turn Kathleen's mind from thoughts of panic and death, to joy and life. She cannot be confronted on the street. Max, Micah and I must wait until she is in Dr. Porter's office, as his destiny is entwined with hers. We follow her out of the alley and make it onto a slightly more travelled thoroughfare, keeping several shop windows between us.

Once again, the spiritual world merges into the temporal earthly realm and we are able to see the demonic forces that are attempting to derail her destiny and the destiny of hundreds of thousands of people in East Africa and India. They are everywhere and they are angry at the invasion of Heaven on Earth. They appear as frogs standing three feet tall with the bones of men's fingers through their noses and tiny red jewels in their foreheads. Their jaws are massive, and mouths are filled with pointed teeth. They can speak, their voices soft and musical, like the sirens that lured sailors to their doom, hypnotic and lulling to a false peace. They are the territorial spirits of Witchcraft, Poverty and Idolatry over different parts of the world and they are here protecting their territories.

All around the frog spirits begin to transform. They constrict like serpents writhing on the ground attempting to coil around their prey to squeeze the life out of them. As people in poverty are fearful about their next meal and distracted by the cares of this life, the snakes slowly constrict, tightening and compressing until there is no room for chest movement to take the next breath. Their breath is literally squeezed out of them.

The Principality of Death in his blackened shroud watches overhead and his dark angelic entourage fill the skies like vultures waiting for the kill to devour the remains.

I hear Bennett's words in my spirit, "The battle is not yours, but the Lord's".

The battle begins to rage between the angelic and the demonic. Swords are clashing furiously. The Lord's angels are out in force with a sword in one hand and a shield in the other. The heads of serpents and frogs are beginning to litter the street. I begin to sing praises to the Lord under my breath, whispering prayers and thanking the Lord for His heavenly host. Max and Micah engage with the angelic hosts as I think to myself that the war being raged on this seedy street at this time in the world's history is incongruous.

I am more and more aware that the battle has raged every day since the fall of Adam and Eve in the Garden. The people of Earth have been believers in only what they could see, not what is in reality. The spiritual realm, both good and evil, has determined earthly reality for millennium and what is seen is only the tip of the iceberg. Nearly all the battle is taking place in the unseen realm. How would world events have played out if mankind had been aware of the spiritual realm and made a conscious choice to agree with Heaven for their futures? I wonder.

My pace quickens, trying to catch up to Kathleen. The streets are fairly crowded, and I see Kathleen's face and then lose her as another corner is turned. She darts in and out of doorways looking over her shoulder, fear on her face. The people on the street have noticed the chase. It is a rare sight to see a woman running on the street and on this street, there are two, one obviously chasing the other. Faces are curious, but no one is attempting to help Kathleen or stop me. Suddenly, I realize that I am once again in front of Dr. Porter's office, a place I recognized from the movie frames. Not sure exactly where Kathleen is, I enter the office to wait. This is Kathleen's planned destination and instead of following her on the outside, I will wait for her inside.

I walk through the door with Max and Micah following. Kathleen has already arrived. The door that I saw close behind her in the window views, is beginning to close now, with Kathleen led into the exam room and Dr. Porter's hand on the doorknob. This is the exact moment for which I have come. I have journeyed over the sea and one hundred years into the past for Kathleen and for her destiny and I will not be thwarted, nor will God's plan for her life.

I burst through the door and Kathleen lets out a little shriek, as she believed that she had lost us in the seedy streets of London. Dr. Porter is aghast that anyone would invade the privacy of an exam room. But fear is in his eyes, as well as guilt, for he knows the reason why Kathleen is here. Though abortion is widely accepted and there are many such "doctors," it is not legal and what he has participated in has not always worked for the mother's good. He has begun to wonder whether he is in the right place in his life.

Jesus' words begin to pour into my spirit, and I hear His voice and the words He would speak to Kathleen. The words are not mine, nor do I need to fear what I need to say to Kathleen to change her mind. Kathleen's destiny is not in my hands, but in the Lord's. What I hear in my spirit, I say to Kathleen. *"Kathleen Mary, the Lord has sent me on a great journey to speak with you. Do not fear. Your destiny is still before you; as is the destiny of the daughter inside your womb. Do not be rid of her, for in so doing your own destiny will end today as well. Be strong in Me, says the Lord.*

Do not be deceived into thinking that your life is over because of what has happened to you. For it is now that your life will be changed forever. Soon you will meet a man of God, one that I put before you, who will be smitten with you all of your days. Together you will touch the hurting and lost within the spiritually darkest nations on Earth. It will become your life's passion, and that of your children, your children's children and their children. Your legacy will be one of hope, compassion and My love to people who would have been lost for eternity. Revel in it and know that I love you and am with you always.

Your descendants will be like you, primarily women, and each will wear your mark. Each daughter will have a small mark like a strawberry on her cheek just as you wear. Regardless of the surname taken in marriage, this mark reveals your lineage, Kathleen Mary McDonald—a lineage of daughters, and is an outward promise that I will keep my word and bless your offspring all their days as a result of your obedience today."

As Priscilla watches Kathleen, her facial expressions change from fear, to disbelief, to hope and then joy as the Holy Spirit witnesses this truth in her spirit. Tears fall down her cheeks even as she smiles and laughs in joy.

Dr. Porter wipes his face with a handkerchief, also in tears, feeling the hope in my words to Kathleen. He is grateful that God looks on the women who come into his office and is ashamed at what He knows God has seen him do over the course of many years. Though he doesn't know the Lord well, he was a believer in his youth. He feels the need to be rescued from the role he has put himself in, the one of executioner of innocents and the remover of the hope of future generations.

Suddenly, he sees a three-dimensional view of time, and the knowledge that as one generation is removed, so, too, are the ones who would come after it. He has contributed to empty future generations all over London.

The Lord has a word for Dr. Porter, as well.

"Thelonius Porter, know this. Before I made the world and everything in it, I saw you. I know your heart. It is time to stop solving problems out of the recesses of your own mind and seek Me, as I can do all things. I have shown you a picture of generational consequences. Heed the revelation and know that I can make all things new—in your life and in those you treat. Let them know that I see them, I know them, and catch every tear they cry. I have them on a path and if they put their trust in Me, they will never be disappointed. I love you and those you hold dear. For several weeks you have been unsure of your current path and felt no joy in your vocation. Your spirit has been asking if you are in the right place and if this is all there is to life. I have been talking with you, Spirit to spirit.

Your life is going to take a change in course, as you have asked. No longer will you be disillusioned by the call you have accepted for your own life, but you will accept My call on your life. Love your patients and pray with them. Your life, instead of dissolving into shame, loss, and death, will follow in a parallel position to that of Kathleen Mary's and her husband's. Prepare to treat people who have never before seen a doctor and minister the truth of My healing to the sick and infirm as well as those who are spiritually dead. Walk with Me and your life will be filled with joy and purpose. Your family has been slowly awakening to a new reality and has been waiting for the change to occur in you. Today that change has arrived. Walk in it and seek

Me for your very life. You will experience life in ways you could never have imagined."

Kathleen Mary stands and she and Dr. Porter embrace, looking at each other as equals in the Kingdom of God, each with a unique calling and purpose, but intertwined. Kathleen lets herself out of the exam room and puts her coat and hat on. As she exits the building, her eyes still wet and her smile joyful. She steps out of the doorway and into a young man walking by in a hurry. He apologizes and looks into her face, immediately smitten. He takes her arm and says that no lady should be walking unescorted in this neighborhood. He introduces himself as a pastor on the way to his first assignment. She laughs.

I am taken up and forward into the future, blessed to see the fruit of this redemption. The vision of Kathleen Mary, her husband, Dr. Porter and all their generations are seen again in windows of time as I quickly pass through it back to my own life. I see Kathleen's wedding, the birth of their daughter, the journey to East Africa, the villages to which they are assigned by God, the daughter's life, wedding, and assignments to Africa and India. Each window of vision breaks up into colored sand and blows away as the next window of time appears.

Finally, my journey swirling through light, is complete and I arrive back in my church in Auckland, Australia. My eyes open and suddenly, standing next to the young man, is a pretty red-haired young woman and she is holding a baby that looks to be about nine months old. My heart starts to beat faster.

The woman is about twenty-six years old and is all I can see. She has lovely red hair and a heart-shaped face. Her face is lit up with joy. My eyes fill with tears as I listen to the Scottish woman talk about her mission. I watch as she comforts her tiny daughter halfway through their presentation.

When church is over, I walk over to meet her. As I approach the front of the church and to the young woman, my heart leaps. Both the red-haired missionary and her infant daughter have tiny strawberry marks on their right cheeks. I realize that this mark not only reveals the lineage of the original woman, Kathleen Mary McDonald, but is a sign to me, as well. God has allowed me to be a witness to the "before and after" of Mary Kathleen McDonald and I am thrilled. Tears of joy stream down my face as I thank her for her faithfulness to her life's assignment.

The young missionary's hand reaches over to the top of my head and touches a loop of chain mail that has been interwoven into my hair. She looks at me squinting, with questions in her eyes. I cannot tell her that it is a part of my armor and that I am as surprised as she is to see it there. She looks me in the eye and nods slightly, seeming to understand.

Bennett whispers to me that the generations since Kathleen are 340 people but that their combined destiny, missions of mercy in Africa and India, have saved more than 2,000,000 people for the Kingdom of God.

I hear the Lord say, *"Thank you, and well done."*

I leave the church and again see how much the Father loves His people, and what the Lord is doing for those who would be His and are not yet. He watches, waits, and pines for them. He arranges divine appointments and sets up divine connections to achieve His purposes on Earth. And most of those purposes are the people who are created in His image. How He longs to be united to them, that none would perish, and all would come to repentance.

CHAPTER 13
THE ROCKS CRY OUT

DAY 17, THURSDAY, AUGUST 27 – T MINUS 23
ISABELLA KRIEGER
CHICAGO, IL

I wake rested, exhilarated and filled with joy. I find myself humming a song as I get ready for work. I turn on the TV to catch a glimpse of the news to see what is happening in the world since yesterday and go to get a cup of coffee. I step out of my bedroom and my hand passes through the doorknob once again and I feel the electric charge of the anointing. I feel the hair on my head and arms stand straight up as I pass through what feels like an electrical charge in the doorway of the room.

I leave my present place and time and I am delivered onto the cliffs of Newport, Rhode Island in present day. I stroll on what is known as the "Cliff Walk" behind the mansions of the Gilded Age, owned by those who made much of their wealth before and during the Industrial Revolution, including such famous families as the Astor's, the Vanderbilt's, and the Duke's. The homes are beautiful "cottages" as the residents have named them, and I wonder if a small percentage of the wealth that built them could have been used differently and made an enormous impact on the world.

On the other side of the Cliff Walk roars the Atlantic Ocean. The waves crash hard and the noise is deafening.

"The sound is amplified here. It is why I chose this place to meet you today."

I turn in surprise, feeling the stratosphere ripple with power.

"I knew that you would love it. Your senses are reeling with the light of the sun, the beauty of the mansions, the sea, and the clouds in the sky. You have always liked sound; soft piano music and fire trucks blowing their horns in parades. The air is filled with the fragrance of the last blooms of roses and the salty smell of the sea."

He is standing right in front of me. His hair blows in the wind and His eyes light with amusement and shine with genuine pleasure. The scent of balsam and frankincense adds to the fragrant mix of the sea and roses that line the path. I breathe in deeply to capture it. He is dressed in jeans, a forest green t-shirt, and sandals, His hair is long, and His beard is perfectly trimmed. How often has he walked amongst us? I wondered. He looks just like one of us.

"Lord!" I bow my head and am tempted to prostrate myself on this cliff walk in worship as I feel the awe of Him.

He takes my hand and says, *"Sit. Please"*.

We sit on the huge rocks and turn to watch the sea. Although it crashes with power against these rocks, I sense far more power in the Man sitting next to me.

"Know the season you are in. It is very short in terms of elapsed time, but it will impact millions of souls. I am talking face-to-face with each of the remnant Light Ops Special Forces troops to thank you and to emphasize the importance of your mission. Remember to pray in the spirit, praise Me, and stay far from strife. Be conscious of yourself and examine your heart, even as you focus on Me and My goodness.

Your assignments were handpicked for you. You are a scribe and you will do more in the spirit than you have ever done and more than anyone else could do for those in your care these next days. Remember to praise and worship Me constantly, as the revealed knowledge of Myself, through worship, brings power to you. It is like oxygen to your bloodstream and your spirit receptors are filled as you carry My Presence to those to whom you are assigned.

The whole natural world praises Me. The stars sing their praises. The trees whisper in time like the fingers of ten thousand stringed instruments. The rocks cry out and clap their hands from morning until evening and evening until morning. The tall grasses and rose bushes swish and undulate in their dance of praise to Me. The birds sing, the ocean ripples and thunders in constant percussion. Can you hear them now? And the whole Earth waits impatiently for the sons of God to be revealed." [26]

He reaches over and gently touches my left ear.

All at once I hear sounds I have never before heard. The sweet melody far away is like the background of a beautiful orchestra. Everything near me—the trees, rose bushes, tall grasses near the cliff walk wall, and the ocean sand and rocks—moves in harmony, some in perfect time and others in solo worship, each in its own rhythm. The most impressive to me is the sound of the rocks. There are huge boulders, large rocks, and the "filler" rocks about six inches in diameter. These smaller rocks clap thunderously. As the water of the ocean crashes over the boulders, it falls on the smaller rocks as the waves retreat back into the sea. The rocks are displaced with every wave and they crash into each other, rock against rock every minute of every day. The sound is as a huge audience clapping in applause as it reverberates throughout the dome of a cathedral, the circle of the Earth.

Suddenly I speak Psalm 148 from memory, though I had never memorized it before today. Never have these words rung so true.

"Hallelujah! Praise the Lord! Let the skies be filled with praise and the highest heavens with the shouts of glory! Go ahead—praise him, all you his messengers! Praise him some more, all you heavenly hosts! Keep it up, sun and moon! Don't stop now, all you twinkling stars of light! Take it up even higher—up to the highest heavens, until the cosmic chorus thunders his praise! Let the entire universe erupt with praise to God. From nothing to something he spoke and created it all. He established the cosmos to last forever, and he stands behind his commands so his orders will never be revoked. Let the earth join in with this parade of praise!

You mighty creatures of the ocean's depths, echo in exaltation! Lightning, hail, snow, and clouds, and the stormy winds that fulfill his word. Bring your melody, O mountains and hills; trees of the forest and field, harmonize your praise! Praise him, all beasts and birds, mice and men, kings, queens, princes, and princesses, young men and maidens, children and babes, old and young alike, everyone everywhere. Let them all join in with this orchestra of praise. For the name of the Lord is the only name we raise!" [27]

I am in awe of Him. And I am amazed by the sounds joining together in perfect worship of the One Who created every participant in this symphony of sound and dance movement. I am a participant as well, as I worship Him with my body, mind, will, emotions, and spirit. I am also conscious, as I have never been before, of the power rushing through me like freshly oxygenated blood through my arteries and veins the more I worship Him.

He looks at me, understanding my thoughts, and smiles.

"Call upon Me in the day of trouble and I will deliver you.[28] I have completely caused every tribulation to be made null and void for you. I will keep him in perfect peace whose mind is stayed on Me.[29] I love you and I AM with you wherever you go."

We stand, and I turn to tell Him again that I love Him. He is gone without a trace. As He departs, I once again hear the movement of the rocks as they clap their hands in the auditorium of this world and then I am gone. I am amazed. I am once again exactly where I was when I left my bedroom, in the hallway leading to my kitchen. The power is so strong in me that my hands shake with it as I decide that today I have no further need for coffee.

In light of where I have just been, and with Whom, the thought of going to work falls short. The only thing that gives it relevance are the thoughts of the people I will encounter, and the urgency of the short time left. I am extremely aware of the swirl of the dark green clouds coming closer as this season of time hastens to a close.

The News show on TV is showing the conflicts around Israel as missiles are hurled in from its borders. Russia, Iran, Turkey and Syria are engaged in talks about Israel's nuclear weapon, their weapon defense systems and access to the Land at the northern border, further widening the chasm between the goat and sheep nations.

I whisper a prayer, "Have Your way, Sir, in the nations of the world. Let there be peace in Jerusalem and protect Your people, Lord."

CHAPTER 14
ΛLTHEΛ

DΛY 18, FRIDΛY, ΛUGUST 28 – T MINUS 22
SOLEDΛD PEREZ (SOLI)
SΛN JOSE, COSTΛ RICΛ

I have slept all through the night and wake up surprised. By this time in my day, I have usually spent hours and sometimes days or even weeks away on my Special Ops assignments. Most have begun in the middle of the night. I am eighteen days into the forty-day assignment and have already been all over the world. But this morning I am getting ready for an ordinary day as if nothing is different in my life.

I am a Sephardic Jew who was born in Costa Rica in 1936. My parents immigrated to Costa Rica from Poland two years before I was born. I am the first of three children and this has been my home all of my life. Had my parents stayed in Poland, I likely would have had my life cut short as World War II began two years later and Germany invaded Poland in 1939.

I have been married and widowed twice—the first when I was only 28 years old and the second in my sixty-sixth year. I was eight months pregnant when Gabe, my husband of nine years, was killed in a fishing accident. My two children stayed with my mother as the shock of his death immediately caused me to enter into early labor, my body and mind heaving in pain from the loss. My delivery was long and arduous, contractions hard and merciless, but without progress. As I weakened, both my unborn child and I were distressed. When the bleeding began, I began to lose consciousness. It was then that I had a visitation by the Lord Jesus, Himself, and converted in the spirit from Judaism to Christianity. Miraculously, minutes later, my youngest son was born in perfect condition and my own recovery was swift with no need for the Rabbi that had been called to give me the Jewish equivalent of last rites.

My second marriage was four years later to a wonderful warm and kind believer. He loved my three children and me and passed away after 35 years of marriage of a massive heart attack. I have had my adult children and their children to give me company and joy but as I have neared my 85th birthday, I have been longing to be finished with my life in the earth realm and to join my husband and my Savior. My evening on the mountain with the Lord, the angel, and the others who have been called for the last day's missions have brought me purpose, joy and strength. Even my appearance has changed as I have traveled laterally over the earth on assignment and backward in time. I have lost years and I look like I am in my forties rather than mid-eighties and my eyes sparkle with my secrets.

I couldn't actually see them, of course, but I know that both of my husbands were in the Great Cloud of Witnesses that evening on the mountain when our deployment was announced to us. I can feel how proud they are of me.

Every morning as I rise from sleep, I feel honored that I have been chosen to fulfill the Lord's purposes in the rescue of the lost. I am living Luke 4:18-19 and am acutely aware that, like Jesus:

> *"The Spirit of the Lord is upon me, and he has anointed me to be hope for the poor, freedom for the brokenhearted, and new eyes for the blind, and to preach to prisoners, 'You are set free!' I have come to share the message of Jubilee, for the time of God's great acceptance has begun."*[30]

After I wash my face and brush my teeth, I run a brush through my hair and put on some lipstick. As I choose an outfit for the day, I continue to wonder how and where the Lord will use me today. I slip into a pair of black slacks and a midnight blue sweater and matching scarf and check my reflection in the mirror. As I look at my reflection, I see my image begin to move and ripple as if I am looking at myself through a deep pool of water. My likeness appears to be undulating, surrounded by the mirror's frame of gold. I can't resist it and feel drawn to touch the mirror to see what it is made of … is it glass or is it something else?

My fingers move into the mirror and are immediately lost to my sight. I feel in my fingertips the sensation of sound waves pulsing, although I can't hear anything. I put the rest of my arm into the reflection as far as it will go, discerning that I won't know where I am going until I pass completely though the "door" that is the mirror. I follow my hand and step completely through the mirror.

Isabella observes as Soli moves through the mirror to her appointed assignment and begins to record.

It is 7:30 on Friday morning in my real life. But my watch tells me that it is 10:13 p.m. on Sunday night, September 7, 1952. I find myself in the French Quarter of New Orleans, Louisiana. The night is warm and muggy, and the smells of Bourbon Street are pungent, a blend of pleasant food smells mixed with those that indicate chains of captivity. My nose is assaulted by cigarette smoke, the smell of stale beer and the faint but noxious smell of vomit wafting from an alleyway. The street is very crowded, filled with tourists, restaurateurs, shopkeepers and bouncers—a mix of insiders and outsiders in The Big Easy.

I look up suddenly as a shaft of reflected light hits my eyes and see what those with natural eyes cannot. The mirror portal hangs over my head at a third story level and I can see hundreds of people crowding the street in it. Though we are relatively far away from the face of the mirror, I can easily pick out myself, and the angels who accompany me everywhere. I see myself, once again at my heavenly age of 33 years old, fully clothed in silver armor and carrying a brilliant sword that not only catches and reflects the dim light present on the street but generates light all of its own. In a circle around me, about four feet on all sides, are seven ten-foot angels of light and they, too, are fully outfitted in armor. I take my eyes away from the mirror and turn to look around myself. The seven angels surrounding me have the appearance of men and women of normal height, wearing black, olive or white t-shirts and jeans. They look to be traveling on foot in a sea of people who desire for a night or two to experience the darkness and secrets of New Orleans, Louisiana.

I am being pushed and shoved, moved up the street by the crowd. My eyes focus on a woman staggering toward me about seventy feet ahead. A dark-skinned white man with Creole ancestry is pulling the woman forcefully down the street, partly because of her drugged state and partly because she is unwilling to go where he wants her to go. As their approach draws nearer, I see that the woman would have been truly lovely were it not for her vacant and hopeless eyes. Her face looks like it has been ravaged by time, but she can't be any older than 21 or 22. Her complexion is dull and pale.

She is wearing a sheer blue blouse with puffed sleeves and nothing under it. She wears black, very short shorts and black fishnet stockings under them. Her feet are shod in high heels, but she can barely stay upright in them. Her dark hair is unkempt but clean, her complexion pale, her nose pierced with a tiny ring and her full lips are in a straight line. It feels as if it has been a long time since this woman smiled with real joy. She is obviously under the influence of a very strong drug, which has numbed her mind, will and emotions. Her body seems to move forward of its own volition in obedience to the man whose hand pulls her by the arm. We converge at a crossroad, at the corner of Bourbon and St. Anne Streets, not far from Jackson Square.

Although people are pressing both of them from all four directions, she suddenly becomes aware of me. Her eyes, a beautiful green, suddenly open wide and focus on me, eye to eye. We have of course, never met, never seen each other, but she has the look of recognition on her face. She stares at me for a few seconds before turning her head slightly to regard the man who is pulling her forward, trying to get her in her state of stupor, to hurry. Her expression becomes filled with a variety of emotions. Fear, hopelessness, grief, shame, dread, and finally resolution pass like shadows over her features, one right after the other. She looks at me again, her eyes once more become glassy and empty. The woman and the man pass and are gone, enveloped by the crowd.

She is the one I am here for, and as I turn to follow, I am filled with personal and ancestral knowledge of this woman. Once again, I am able to view the life of another as a moving picture shot from more than 200 years before to this woman's present.

Her path has been formed by a bloodline of ancestral betrayal, slavery, rape, prostitution, witchcraft and addiction. A cyclic pathway with ruts so deep, it has been impossible for her to climb out. Were it not for a childhood commitment to the Lord when she was taken under the wing of a young friend's mother, she might be lost forever. My assignment is to be the Lord's answer to the prayers she uttered as a little girl, to rescue her from the curses in her bloodline and set her back on the course God had her on to meet both her own destiny and to influence the others He put in her true path.

The first picture of the woman's genealogy takes place in the year 1782 and I am watching a scene of terror as Bennett speaks into my ear. "We are observing a man and woman running in the darkness in Cameroon, West Africa. We are hearing the voices of other people running too and of those chasing them."

The woman is caught first, and the man stops when he hears her screams. Turning back to help her, they both are captured and led away violently in chains. Their skin is dark, and they are soaked in sweat, but his fearful and hopeless expressions match those of his great-great-great-great-great granddaughter in the French Quarter of a city thousands of miles and two centuries away.

The next scene is aboard a sailing ship as the deck moves up and down over the swells of the sea. The sails are filled with wind and there are miles of ocean ahead. Even as the seas roar and the winds howl, I can hear the muted cries of people below deck. Two levels below are people shoulder to shoulder. Those around the periphery are manacled at the wrist to the sides of the ship, the ones in the center by the ankle. The air is hot, and the odor is indescribable, filled with the smells of excrement, vomit, disease, rotting flesh, fear and death. The man and woman are at opposite ends but watch each other as if they are each other's only hope to finish the journey alive.

The ship has landed at Alexandria, Virginia and the captives have been removed to a slave house in the center of the old town, to be fattened up and restored after the arduous journey across the Atlantic Ocean. Who would purchase a half dead slave, after all? From there, they will travel to New Orleans, Louisiana, where they will be paraded on a slave block to be sold to the highest bidder. The two are fortuitously sold to the same French landowner and moved to a plantation twenty miles away.

The pictures begin to move quickly like a deck of cards being shuffled. The new master has taken notice of the woman's beauty and her quiet defiance. At first, she works in the fields picking cotton, side by side with her husband and the other slaves. Her back aches and her hands are rough and bleeding but at least they are together.

After a time, her owner moves her into the outdoor kitchen, away from her husband and closer to the house where he can keep an eye on her. She is fearful of him and begins to form an alliance with another slave, an older woman who has been on this property for more than twenty years. She is also from West Africa and has brought with her indigenous knowledge of spells, curses, and incantations. She uses a small rag doll that she has fashioned out of sticks, cotton, and scraps of fabric as a substitute "master".

Soon, the woman's fears are realized when he brings her into the home to assist the other house servants. He cleans her up, dresses her in a uniform, and puts her into the tutelage of a woman slave only a couple of years her senior. She begins to stay in the house at night instead of in the slave quarters outside where her husband lives. One night after an evening where the master has imbibed on Kentucky bourbon since mid-afternoon, he visits her room. It is the start of many nights where he claims her as his in every way. Soon she becomes pregnant and cannot meet the eyes of the other slaves or those of her husband.

Once again, she visits the old woman who possesses the doll substitute and they begin to use it to punish the master of the plantation, their owner. She continues to work all day and be used during the night. She bears a little girl with creamy dark skin, much lighter than both her mother and her mother's husband. There is no doubt from whence this child came.

Meanwhile, the master has become ill.

As her life passes quickly before my eyes, I witness the master's death by a slow and wasting disease and the child's growth and development. The child grows into a lovely woman whose innocence is taken in the same way as her mother's, at the age of fourteen. The doll is used once again as another master dies, and another child is conceived and born. The cycle occurs again twice more, and time passes through the Civil War and the abolition of slavery.

The fourth-generation woman child, conceived in rape is now "free" from slavery and works in a fine home as a servant, however the cycle continues. She has attracted the attention of the rich man of the house and the generations before her have taught her to use her beauty to survive and to thrive. He removes her from the home he shares with his wife and children and into a home of her own where his visits are not witnessed by those he loves. She, too, conceives a child and the man supports two families. As she ages, she loses some of the beauty that has been her security, and he abandons her and their child to the street. He then takes possession of the house she has lived in for fifteen years. They are "taken in" by a brothel in the seediest part of New Orleans where she begins to work as a prostitute for their room and board. Through it all, the doll is used to curse, punish and gradually kill the men responsible for controlling, raping, and securing a much less than desirable future for the women and their daughters conceived in shame.

The fifth and sixth generations follow this same path of prostitution, a different face of slavery and female babies born into it. Curses are whispered over the dolls and several cruel and heartless men die, wasting away. Voodoo is a regional and territorial spirit that follows these women and is represented by the queen of voodoo, Marie Laveau. Laveau is high and lifted up as the representative of a regional stronghold of witchcraft and voodoo. I see her face and that of Jezebel as they sit in their golden and jeweled thrones in the skies over Louisiana. In addition to these queens of rebellion, manipulation, and control, is a male spirit, the principality of religion. The French Cajun people and slaves brought here against their will years ago have interwoven religion and witchcraft for centuries and their spiritual kings and queens are holding court here tonight.

Roi Pape de Légalisme et le Traditionalisme Religieux, as he calls himself, is dressed all in white robes with a tall pointed papal tiara on his head and a large gold and ruby ring on the forefinger of his right hand. He is the king and priest of legalism and traditional religion. He has the final say on religious law. He has been around for millennia and on his decrees and judgment people have been drowned, burned at the stake, and drawn and quartered. There is no choice really for he "only does what he must".

Marie Laveau was a black woman of African descent and tonight she is wearing a white sleeveless dress that shows her voluptuous shape, her black hair pulled high and covered by a bright red headscarf. Her lips are bright red and the whites of her eyes shine with an unnatural light. Around her neck are many jeweled necklaces and her ears are decorated with large gold-hooped earrings. A large snake hugs itself around her neck and slithers down her right arm to her wrist. Her home while she walked the earth is not far from where we are now. Her grave is a whitewashed above-ground tomb covered with black x's and surrounded by the offerings of captivated visitors to New Orleans— empty rum bottles, beer cans, stuffed animals, small dolls, cigarette butts, dead flowers and filth. Their memorabilia reflect their slavery to addiction and to the one that presides over the city, the queen of voodoo. Her throne is a golden high-backed chair encrusted with emeralds and rubies and she stretches herself on it like a sleek cat, anticipating what she will see on this evening. At her feet is the doll that is used as the accursed human substitute.

Jezebel is a white woman with long dark hair. She, too, is voluptuous and beautiful, but she is dressed in a form-fitting black pinstriped business suit, black sheer stockings and red stiletto heels. Her throne is an elegant, red winged-back chair with a golden pillow behind her back, covered in pearls and topaz beads. She is a spirit that has been manipulating and controlling people through the ages, since her namesake walked the earth as queen of Israel, wife of King Ahab, in Elijah's day. She was a worshipper of Baal and mocked the God of Israel. Unlike Marie Laveau, she has no tomb anywhere on Earth. As prophesized by Elijah, dogs ate her dead body—all except her skull, her feet and the palms of her hands.

Bennett, the angel in the war room of Heaven, whispers the name of the woman I have been following, "Althea." Althea is the seventh generation of the couple chased in the jungle of West Africa. She is the seventh-generation slave and the seventh generation to the mix of witchcraft and religion in this part of the world. The number seven represents completion. Enough is enough!

I witness the young woman's life since birth in the moving pictures of Althea's life. I observe Althea's mother filled with hope even as she prostitutes herself. I watch as I see them spoken to repeatedly by a kind woman in New Orleans, on the street, in the grocery store, and "by chance" in front of a church as mother and small child walk by. The mother continues in her ways, doing her best to provide for her young daughter, and trusting the woman who is gradually befriending her. Althea meets the woman's daughter and they become friends. The woman reads to the two girls out of a picture book of Bible stories and talks to them about Jesus. The woman's daughter knows all about Him and tells Althea, too, as they play. Althea believes what she hears and accepts Jesus as her Lord when she is about ten years old.

One day Althea's mother drops her eleven-year-old daughter off at the church with the kind woman and leaves, promising to come back later in the day to pick her up. She never returns. There is not a trace of her except for a few belongings in the small and dingy apartment that mother and daughter have shared since Althea was small. The kind woman's intentions are good as she calls the authorities to try to find Althea's mother, but Althea is now a ward of the State of Louisiana and is put into foster care.

I continue to watch Althea's story and see her shuffled from house to house in the foster system. In three of the six houses she lives in during the seven years until her eighteenth birthday, foster fathers, brothers and teenage foster boys have sexually molested her. In this moving picture, with and without Althea in it, these men and boys are wasting away over time, dying slowly and painfully, sick, thin, and covered with sores.

Althea is moved from house to house. The sexual slavery assignment on her family line continues and on Althea's eighteenth birthday, she is expelled from her last limited security foster home into the seamy streets of New Orleans. She remembers her mother's life and the stories of her grandmother and great-grandmother. She feels destined to live the same life and enters that life purposefully, feeling as though this time she is doing something by choice, rather than by force. She takes what is left of her mother's meager life and moves into an apartment run by a man who offers to help her. This man is the same man who is dragging Althea through the Bourbon Street area this very evening. He starts her on drugs to numb her body and her mind, knowing that soon she will be unable to leave by choice. She will work for him by selling her body and he will keep her imprisoned by heroin addiction.

Foot traffic is congested, and they are unaware that they are being followed. That same street congestion is making it difficult for the angels and me to keep up with them.

After three blocks of running west on Bourbon Street, past Orleans Avenue, St. Peter and Toulouse Streets, the couple turns north on St. Louis toward the St. Louis Cemetery, hoping to escape into the night and blend with the sightseers and true worshippers of darkness who converge there. All around me I can hear the sounds of torment as we near the St. Louis Cemetery No.1, which covers one square block. It holds thousands of sinners and saints beginning in 1789 including industry giants, such as Etienne de Bore (a pioneer of the sugar industry), Homer Plessy (the plaintiff in the 1896 civil rights case), Barthelemy Lafon (architect turned pirate for Jean LaFitte), Delphine LaLaurie (the notoriously cruel slave owner), along with many famous politicians and aristocrats.

I can hear the sounds of warfare in the skies, swords crashing against one another and, for the first time it appears that the couple we are following can hear them, too. Lightening streaks out of dark clouds just above us, the sky's ceiling is a short one tonight.

There are several people up ahead surrounding one of the mausoleums and they are reverent in their stance. Bennett whispers, "Some are truly worshippers of Marie Laveau and have chosen the dark side. Others are here for the mystery. They love the feeling of fear and even terror. It drives them in a search for more. Tonight, they will see the demonic and it will forever change them to seek only after the Light."

I have smelled bad odors in my lifetime, like burning cheese that has fallen off my frozen pizza onto the floor of the oven or burned popcorn

... or roadkill on a country road in 90-degree heat. The supernatural smell of death here is overpowering and although only I can smell it right now, everything is about to change. Soon everyone will be gagging.

The ground begins to shake slightly and Althea and her "escort" suddenly stop running, afraid they will fall. Those chanting near Laveau's grave are still as well, eyes filled with fear. Suddenly the earth quakes more violently. It lasts for several seconds as gravestones and mausoleums begin to roll over onto their sides. The earth forms a chasm between the headstones and intense heat pours out of the ground. The crevice is about ten feet deep, thirteen feet long and six feet wide. Everyone looks over the side, being careful not to fall in as the ground continues to move with aftershocks. Fire shoots up to nearly ground level, but it is not the fire that is holding the attention of everyone watching. There are hundreds of living, blackened and charred bodies intermingled with serpents below the ground. The voices from the bodies are moaning and shrieking in pain and hopelessness.

In an instant, I remember the story of Lazarus and the rich man in Luke 16.[31] I know this is a night of grace for all who are here, in spite of how it looks right now. Lazarus was a poor beggar who sat at the gate to the city every day begging for money and food. The rich man walked by every day in his fine purple robes and ignored the plight of Lazarus. Lazarus even sat begging on the steps of the rich man's opulent home, impossible to ignore.

In time, both the rich man and Lazarus died. The rich man went to Hell and Lazarus to paradise, held in Abraham's bosom. The rich man looked up and saw Abraham. He was in agony and requested that Lazarus come down with a cool drop of water on his fingertip to quench the fire and thirst in his mouth, but Abraham said the chasm between Heaven and Hell could not be crossed. The rich man said that he understood that he could not go back to his life but asked if Lazarus could be raised to show himself to his five brothers.

> "So, the rich man said, 'Then let me ask you, Father Abraham, to please send Lazarus to my relatives. Tell him to witness to my five brothers and warn them not to end up where I am in this place of torment.'
>
> "Abraham replied, 'They've already had enough warning. They have the teachings of Moses and the prophets, and they must obey them.'
>
> "'But what if they're not listening?' the rich man added. 'If someone from the dead were to go and warn them, they would surely repent.'
>
> "Abraham said to him, 'If they won't listen to Moses and the prophets, neither would they believe even if someone was raised from the dead!'" [32]

The people who are looking into the shallow abyss are being given another chance. They are seeing Hell first-hand. It is a real place with real people paying real consequences for sin and unbelief. Of the fifteen here, two are Satanists and will not repent. The rest have dabbled and experimented and have played where it is not safe. They know it now.

Suddenly, a large snake slithers from behind the headstones and, transformed, rises to his thirteen-foot height. He is a dark angel dressed in black with huge black wings. His head is bald, his eyes black in a totally pale white face, no lashes or brows. His nose looks like it has been cut off with only thin skin over bones and sinuses. His lips are full, and his mouth is grimacing in hatred at the men and women that God created who are viewing his failures.

The seven angels who surround me are each his equal in power and he knows it. There are at least seven more angels who are surrounding Althea. Each angel is twelve to fifteen feet tall and is dressed in full armor with huge swords drawn. Althea and the man who has dragged her around the French Quarter for the past eighteen months, prostituting her and keeping her supplied with heroin to keep her compliant, are standing several feet apart. Her face is filled with peace and his is distorted in terror.

The thirteen who are not interested in a life where Satan rules and reigns, are looking at me, recognizing I have a special role in this place, as does Althea. Perhaps it is the angels … they are difficult to miss.

I shout, "Choose this day whom you will serve. Tonight, you have seen true darkness and the one who rules it. Tonight, you have seen Hell. It is a gift to you and to whom much is given much is required. Please take notice. Jesus is not an excluder; He does not inspire fear; He is not a hater. I have come at the order of the King of kings and Lord of lords who came to earth in love … with you. I say again, choose this day Whom you will serve. Will you choose Jesus of Nazareth? Or will you choose any other god, which will ultimately leave you in the company of the Devil in the pit of fire for eternity? The choice has always been yours!"

The chasm closes like a sutured wound as suddenly as it opened, but the scar will remain as a reminder to those who were here tonight and to all they will tell about it. The air is becoming fresh and clean, and the smells of death and decay are beginning to dissipate. The old cemetery remains innocuous, beautiful and historic, neither good nor evil. All have chosen wisely and are now following us out of the cemetery to Jackson Square where we will sit for hours. Fear is seductive and deceptive. Shalom peace replaces it tonight. Honest, open, with nothing missing and nothing broken. It brings relief to those of us whose eyes have shifted from the dark angel to the Man of Peace, Jesus. It pleasures me greatly that they are drawn like a moth to a flame to Jesus and His goodness, not because of fear but because of His love.

"Althea, you are my assignment for tonight. The Lord has seen your bloodline and the seven generations in one form of slavery or another. Tonight, the bondage of slavery ends forever. It is for liberty that Christ set us free[33] and whom the Son sets free is free indeed[34]. No more selling your body. Your body is His Temple.[35] No more voodoo dolls and curses spoken over the men who have hurt you. Forgive and repent, for the Kingdom of Heaven is truly at hand."

I hear the voice of the Lord Himself speaking to Althea:

"I have swept away your sins like a thick cloud. I have made your guilt vanish like mist disappearing into thin air. Now come back, come back to me, for I have paid the price for you." [36]

"Tonight, go back to the church your mother used to take you to when you were very young. You will meet the woman you knew and her daughter. God has spoken to them and they have been praying for you for days. They have been told by the Lord to expect you and will be delighted when you ring their bell tonight. They have a warm bed for you and will facilitate everything you need to start your new life. Your destiny is great, and many will come to the Lord as a result of you. Go and be blessed."

Althea's drug dealer and pimp, a man named Franco also comes to the Lord tonight. His fear finally goes as he is filled with the love of God. He, too, has a destiny to be achieved, defined before the world was created and one that will now be realized.

The seven angels and I leave Jackson Square. One by one, each of us fades. I suddenly find myself back in my bedroom, lipstick in hand in front of my mirror. My hazel eyes are sparkling, and I see a woman looking back at me who is filled with joy.

"Thank you, Lord", I murmur, feeling blessed to have a place in His end time army.

CHAPTER 15
GOG'S FORAY

DAY 20, SUNDAY, AUGUST 30 – T MINUS 20
ISABELLA KREIGER
CHICAGO, IL

I am again in the War Room of Heaven, Trent and Christopher are at my side and I am watching our Special Forces at work all over the globe. Some are ministering to a single person, their only target for the day, while others are changing the courses of nations. I have a sense of heightened urgency and determination today. My eyes keep returning to the monitor and holograms that observe spiritual and national progress in Israel. There is much work being done throughout the world but the signs of the times and the lines being drawn in the sand are in the Middle East.

In an instant, we are standing on Mount Carmel, just a little over an hour northwest of Jerusalem. Known now for its peaceful scenery and beautiful garden, this is the place where Elijah called down fire on a waterlogged wooden sacrifice in a contest with 450 prophets of Baal.

Whose God would burn up a sacrifice? The Baal prophets danced around waving sticks and calling out to their god, who of course could not hear them. It is difficult for wood and stone to hear when people speak to them. Elijah and the God of Israel won the contest and Elijah slew the 450 prophets of Baal at the brook Kishon.

I gaze down the mountain to Megiddo, the place where Armageddon will be fought. My gaze rises up to the skies. The whole expanse is filled with ropes of clouds in shades of military green and dark gray. The demonic hordes are marching in orderly rows in the heavenlies and they are getting nearer and nearer to their target, the Lord's Beautiful Country.

This is an earthquake zone. The Carmel Fault line splays like fingers on a hand off the Dead Sea Fault line and continues northwest to the Mediterranean Sea. It has been giving warning tremors over the past twenty days, almost as though it knows what is happening in the nations surrounding the nation of Israel. The tectonic plates are putting on their weapons, getting ready for war.

The earth here is quiet. *Deafeningly* quiet. There is not a bird, deer or wild goat in sight. Suddenly, I feel a slight tremor, like a small shock and then tiny ripples following. I feel it in the Spirit, as the epicenter of the quake that is coming will be about twenty miles from here, nearer to the Sea of Galilee.

Suddenly, as quickly as I arrived, I am back in the War Room of Heaven observing what couldn't be seen from my place on Mount Carmel.

The ground level looks very similar to the skies. The demons on the ground match the numbers of human soldiers from the nations of Russia, Libya, Somalia, Sudan, Turkey and Iran. The ground itself looks like it is alive, teaming with activity, both natural and supernatural. Tanks, thousands of troops, rocket launchers, tents and even horses dot the ground, looking like individual pixels in a Georges Seurat impressionistic painting. Only this "painting" is not one of beauty but of an immense coiled snake ready to strike! In the air, there are green helicopters for battle and black helicopters filming the destruction to deliver the news to the world. Their excitement is tangible. In the Mediterranean Sea, there is the outline of a large submarine who will deliver its nuclear payload to ensure that Israel is truly wiped off the map.

Jesus walks in and says,

"It is time.

The nations have gathered on every side, on the ground, in the waters, and in the skies above Israel and they are promising her destruction. Hamas and Hezbollah are partying in the streets, even as they are removing their elite government and military leaders from harm's way. The regular people are dispensable but all, Jew and Palestinian alike, are filled with fear at what they see. There are bomb shelters built in every large building and neighborhood. Iran has promised and delivered on the nuclear bombs that have been threatened for decades. There is no defense for those, other than the multi-tiered missile defense system, Iron Dome.

Many are beginning to call upon the name of the Lord and I will answer them. My initial response will be today. While the world will consider My response catastrophic, not one hair on the head of any of My people will be touched. The News agencies will cover it hard for five days or so but they will be unimpressed with the lack of death statistics to report. Angels have been deployed to evacuate the area and there will be none, Jew or Palestinian, in the path of the destruction about to begin.

Russia and its leader—Gog—will understand, however as the Russian President has been reading the Book of Ezekiel for himself, much like Herod the Great did when he told the magi the place of my birth from prophecies written centuries ago. When he reads about this earthquake and sees what is prophesied beyond it, he will shake his fist at Me, the God of the Universe, and continue to move forward with his destructive plans."

I run to the enormous Bible in the center of the large table of opened books of the Lord and begin to read aloud from Ezekiel 38:18-21.

> *"It will come about on that day, when Gog comes against the land of Israel," declares the Lord God, "that My fury will mount up in My anger. In My zeal and in My blazing wrath I declare that on that day there will surely be a great earthquake in the land of Israel. The fish of the sea, the birds of the heavens, the beasts of the field, all the creeping things that creep on the earth, and all the men who are on the face of the earth will shake at My presence; the mountains also will be thrown down, the steep pathways will collapse and every wall will fall to the ground. I will call for a sword against him on all My mountains," declares the Lord God. "Every man's sword will be against his brother."* [37]

The Lord is angry, and His eyes are flashing. Nothing takes Him by surprise. He knows everything there is to know already. Still He is furious with the demonic leaders of the strongholds over Russia, Iran, Turkey, Sudan, Somalia, and Libya for their hatred against Israel. He is especially angry at the ambitious leader of Russia, the spirit of antichrist and the Prince of Persia.

Suddenly, the monitors reveal a shaking in the camera as the view of Israel shows ground movement throughout the nation. The sound, even from the heavenly War Room is deafening. The agitation of the earth continues for about thirty seconds when the movement is ramped up.

The ground from the Sea of Galilee from the north, south, east and west is shaking as the tectonic plates beneath it are moving up and down, causing Seismic waves that are displacing the ground above them. I can see fissures forming, a huge chasm along the fault line. Streets are buckling. The land is absorbing into itself what seconds ago stood upon it.

Abruptly, the tops of four mountaintops that I recognize, Mount Tabor, Mount Carmel, Mount Hermon and Mount Arbel begin to implode, top to bottom, they crack and fall straight down, like the walls of Jericho so long ago, shortening each by more than half. The displacement of enormous rock formations shifts the massive boulders high into the air, each falling like enormous sledgehammers onto other parts of the earth in their vertical downward paths. The mountaintops fall, flattening the rocky topography that has been in place for thousands—even millions— of years. Streets disappear, and homes are swallowed up. The few people who live on those mountains, however, are already evacuated and they are safe. The place on Mount Carmel where I stood just minutes ago is now buried under a new mountain of rubble. The noise continues, sounding like it is every bit as angry as Jesus is. I see dust plumes that reach five thousand feet above the highest crag.

The quake in the adjacent nations of Lebanon, Syria, Jordan and Egypt have caused significant damage, further angering regional principalities and fueling the fire of war even as each nation has to deal with their own humanitarian crises. Gog, the Prince of Antichrist and the Prince of Persia lift their feet over the victims, one in the natural and two in the spirit as they hasten ever more quickly toward war.

I look south, praying desperately for Mount Zion, that it remains standing for all the end time prophesies decreed over it, knowing there is no need to worry, as those prophecies will be fulfilled in their totality.

The epicenter of the quake, the Sea of Galilee area, also has significant damage. Miraculously, no one has been killed or injured. The Sea itself only moments ago like a giant bathtub with a third of its water, along with hundreds of fish, are displaced into the surrounding land.

I watch in absolute silence. A silence that continues as I stare at the scene for hours, though the only activity to be observed is the comparatively gentle fall of fine crushed rock as it settles back to Earth with thick dust blown by occasional gusts of wind. Every leaf, limb and square inch of available surface is covered in it.

Wisdom would say that the land and any physical structures that remain standing are unstable. Aftershocks are unpredictable. They are expected but have not yet started. I have seen only two people brave enough to walk near the epicenter of the earthquake in two hours.

The two Witnesses.

The Lord looks over to me, His face grim. He decrees, "It has begun!"

THE END

PREVIEW OF BOOK TWO
LIGHT OPS: THE FINAL FORTY
EZEKIEL'S WAR

CHAPTER 1
AFGHANISTAN

DAY 22, TUESDAY, SEPTEMBER 1 – T MINUS 18
ISAAC SEROTTI "IZZY"
SAN JOSE, CA

ISABELLA KRIEGER:

Isaac Serotti, called "Izzy" by his parents, has just been kissed goodnight and put to bed. This is his first month out of a crib and in a "big boy bed". He is just getting comfortable in his new surroundings and his eyes are closing in sleep.

Izzy is three years old in Earth time, but his spirit man is the same age as Jesus when He overcame death and the grave. It was the man in Izzy that said, "Send me, send me," long before the world was created. And it is that man who will go into the darkness of Afghanistan tonight, hours after he has been put to bed and his parents are sound asleep.

Izzy has been watching his angels, Emma and Daniel, watch over him since the day of his birth. He knows they are with him always and they are there to keep him safe.

Suddenly, he is awake, and he is not in his bed surrounded by the things that make up his young life. He is outside in bone chilling cold and it is very dark. The new moon is a silver sliver against a clear, cloudless, black sky, lit with only stars. The stars delineate sky from Earth, and he sees gradations and shapes around him, lighter darks and darker darks, and realizes that there are mountain peaks all around.

He stands up to his full six-foot two-inch height, his brown curly hair blowing in the wind. His gray eyes, fully alert, look all around himself in the darkness. It is a very cool feeling to be a toddler, walking into adulthood in two steps. He smiles and walks deeper into the darkness.

Be among the first to know when Book Two is set to release by following Vicki on

Instagram @VickiTaylor0144

A NOTE FROM THE AUTHOR

I hope you have enjoyed *Light Ops: The Final Forty – Signs in the Sky.* Stay tuned for book 2, *Ezekiel's War* and the third in the trilogy, *The New Era,* coming soon.

It is my desire to show the Godhead as they are, not as tradition and stuffy pictures have shown them—stiff, joyless, rigid, and almost bored. We are created in His image. We laugh; we have a sense of humor; we understand irony; we love intensely; we get angry and we weep with sorrow. Where did we get those traits? We got them from the One Who made us *in His image.* He loves us. He wishes that none would perish but He knows those who are His and He has seen the end from the beginning. He knew us before the foundation of the world … a world that He created. He knew the number of our days before there was even one lived. He knew the plans that He had for us. Those who belong to Him have the same destination but not the same earthly destiny.

Light Ops: The Final Forty trilogy shows the special destiny of a few of God's end time warriors. It comes out of my imagination, though I believe He planted it there to show that His purposes can be achieved in different ways than we have been taught by the logic and rules of mankind to believe.

His Kingdom come, His will be done on earth … as it is in heaven,

Vicki Taylor

ABOUT THE AUTHOR

Vicki Taylor is a wife, mother, nurse, entrepreneur, businesswoman, author, humanitarian and ordained minister. Praying for the nations is her passion. This passion led her to travel to countries including Kenya, Tanzania, South Africa, Ethiopia, Israel and Ecuador.

Ordained as a minister of the Gospel of Jesus Christ in 2018, Vicki writes fiction and non-fiction to impact the Kingdom, showing God's love to everyone including those who insist He doesn't exist. She and her husband, Dan, live on the eastern shore of Lake Michigan. They have two grown children and three grandchildren.

VickiATaylor.com

ENDNOTES

1   Simmons, Brian. *The Passion Translation Bible, Romans 13:12.* Bible Gateway, www.biblegateway.com. Accessed 1 Dec. 2019.

2   *New American Standard Bible (NASB), Isaiah 6:8A.* Bible Gateway, www.biblegateway.com. Accessed 10 Nov. 2019.

3   *New American Standard Bible (NASB), Isaiah 6:8B.* Bible Gateway, www.biblegateway.com. Accessed 10 Nov. 2019.

4   Simmons, Brian. *The Passion Translation Bible, Revelation 4:5-11.* Bible Gateway, www.biblegateway.com. Accessed 1 Dec. 2019.

5   *The Holy Bible, Matthew 25 (Paraphrased).* Bible Gateway, www.biblegateway.com. Accessed 15 Oct. 2019.

6   *New American Standard Bible (NASB), Ezekiel 38:1-6.* Bible Gateway, www.biblegateway.com. Accessed 10 Nov. 2019.

7   *New American Standard Bible (NASB), Psalm 14: 1A.* Bible Gateway, www.biblegateway.com. Accessed 10 Nov. 2019.

8   *New American Standard Bible (NASB), Ezekiel 38: 5-6.* Bible Gateway, www.biblegateway.com. Accessed 10 Nov. 2019.

9   Simmons, Brian. *The Passion Translation Bible, Revelation 11:15B.* Bible Gateway, www.biblegateway.com. Accessed 1 Dec. 2019.

10 Simmons, Brian. *The Passion Translation Bible, Revelation 11:15B.* Bible Gateway, www.biblegateway.com. Accessed 1 Dec. 2019.

11 Simmons, Brian. *The Passion Translation Bible, Romans 8: 38-39.* Bible Gateway, www.biblegateway.com. Accessed 1 Dec. 2019.

12 *The Holy Bible, 1 Corinthians 2:16 (Paraphrased)*. Bible Gateway, www.biblegateway.com. Accessed 15 Oct. 2019.

13 *The Holy Bible, 2 Timothy 1:7 (Paraphrased)*. Bible Gateway, www.biblegateway.com. Accessed 15 Oct. 2019.

14 *The Holy Bible, Matthew 24:24 (Paraphrased)*. Bible Gateway, www.biblegateway.com. Accessed 15 Oct. 2019.

15 *The Holy Bible, 1 Samuel 16:7 (Paraphrased)*. Bible Gateway, www.biblegateway.com. Accessed 15 Oct. 2019.

16 *New American Standard Bible (NASB), Genesis 3:1-5*. Bible Gateway, www.biblegateway.com. Accessed 10 Nov. 2019.

17 *The Holy Bible, John 15:13 (Paraphrased)*. Bible Gateway, www.biblegateway.com. Accessed 15 Oct. 2019.

18 *The Holy Bible, Psalm 97:11 (Paraphrased)*. Bible Gateway, www.biblegateway.com. Accessed 15 Oct. 2019.

19 *The Holy Bible, Isaiah 40:4 (Paraphrased)*. Bible Gateway, www.biblegateway.com. Accessed 15 Oct. 2019.

20 *The Holy Bible, Isaiah 52:12 (Paraphrased)*. Bible Gateway, www.biblegateway.com. Accessed 15 Oct. 2019.

21 *The Holy Bible, Psalm 121:4 (Paraphrased)*. Bible Gateway, www.biblegateway.com. Accessed 15 Oct. 2019.

22 *The Holy Bible, Psalm 91:2 (Paraphrased)*. Bible Gateway, www.biblegateway.com. Accessed 15 Oct. 2019.

23 *The Holy Bible, Psalm 138:2 (Paraphrased)*. Bible Gateway, www.biblegateway.com. Accessed 15 Oct. 2019.

24 Simmons, Brian. *The Passion Translation Bible. Acts 9: 1-22*. Bible Gateway, www.biblegateway.com. Accessed 1 Dec. 2019.

25 *New American Standard Bible (NASB), Job 12:13-25*. Bible Gateway, www.biblegateway.com. Accessed 10 Nov. 2019.

26 *The Holy Bible, Romans 8:22 (Paraphrased)*. Bible Gateway, www.biblegateway.com. Accessed 15 Oct. 2019.

27 Simmons, Brian. *The Passion Translation Bible. Psalm 148:1-13.* Bible Gateway, www.biblegateway.com. Accessed 1 Dec. 2019.

28 *The Holy Bible, Psalm 50:15 (Paraphrased)*. Bible Gateway, www.biblegateway.com. Accessed 15 Oct. 2019.

29 *The Holy Bible, Isaiah 26:3 (Paraphrased)*. Bible Gateway, www.biblegateway.com. Accessed 15 Oct. 2019.

30 Simmons, Brian. *The Passion Translation Bible. Luke 4:18-19.* Bible Gateway, www.biblegateway.com. Accessed 1 Dec. 2019.

31 *The Holy Bible, Luke 16:19-27 (Paraphrased)*. Bible Gateway, www.biblegateway.com. Accessed 15 Oct. 2019.

32 Simmons, Brian. *The Passion Translation Bible. Luke 16:27-31.* Bible Gateway, www.biblegateway.com. Accessed 1 Dec. 2019.

33 *The Holy Bible, Galatians 5:1 (Paraphrased)*. Bible Gateway, www.biblegateway.com. Accessed 15 Oct. 2019.

34 *The Holy Bible, John 8:36 (Paraphrased)*. Bible Gateway, www.biblegateway.com. Accessed 15 Oct. 2019.

35 *The Holy Bible, 1 Corinthians 6:19-20 (Paraphrased)*. Bible Gateway, www.biblegateway.com. Accessed 15 Oct. 2019.

36 Simmons, Brian. *The Passion Translation Bible. Isaiah 44:22.* Bible Gateway, www.biblegateway.com. Accessed 1 Dec. 2019.

37 *New American Standard Bible (NASB), Ezekiel 38:18-21.* Bible Gateway, www.biblegateway.com. Accessed 10 Nov. 2019.